Bob Purvis is a retired Head of Modern Languages in a large comprehensive school. Now widowed, he lists as his chief interests music, cricket and his children and grandchildren. He plays the viola as an enthusiastic amateur in an orchestra and chamber groups. Originally from Essex, he is now happily settled in North Yorkshire.

THE TELL-TALE TRIO

A COLLECTION OF SHORT STORIES WITH MUSICAL CONNECTIONS

To all my friends in the Richmondshire Orchestra

Robert Purvis

THE TELL-TALE TRIO

A COLLECTION OF SHORT STORIES WITH MUSICAL CONNECTIONS

AUSTIN MACAULEY
PUBLISHERS LTD.

A CIP catalogue record for this title is available from the British Library.

ISBN 978 184963 393 2

www.austinmacauley.com

First Published (2014)
Austin Macauley Publishers Ltd.
25 Canada Square
Canary Wharf
London
E14 5LB

Printed and Bound in Great Britain

Introduction

Somervell Constantine Geddes B.A. – known to all who could
claim any degree of friendship with him as Velly – although he
had retired from the frenetic and exhausting life of a senior
teacher, still found nevertheless plenty to do to keep both mind
and body just as busy as was congenial to him. He was not one
to pass his days of retirement in armchair-bound idleness, nor
was he so wedded to the idea of work as to be unable to 'wind
down'. He had received during the run-up to his withdrawal
from the rat-race of work a piece of advice that had struck him
at the time as being eminently sensible; an old friend had said
to him, "Whatever you do, make sure you take time off to
smell the roses". Velly had immediately seen the wisdom of
such counsel, and heaven knows he had, over the years, put in
enough hours at his very demanding job to feel perfectly
justified in allowing himself a good rest. There was, he always
said, a balance to be struck between the extremes of total
idleness on the one hand and complete lack of it on the other.
So Velly and Jessie, his wife of forty two years, went about
their daily lives in unhurried but rarely static leisure, taking
pleasure in their children and grandchildren who visited them
regularly, in going out when they felt so inclined, working in
the garden or pottering about the house. Then, when they were
tired, they had the sense and the opportunity to rest and really
enjoy 'smelling the roses'.

Velly Meets Traffy

It was a fine afternoon in late May, one of those days that make you wonder whether, if only the greater part of the summer could be as sunny and cheerful and generally uplifting, the population at large would feel the need to go abroad for its annual ration of 'holiday weather'. Jessie, Velly's wife, had gone off shortly after breakfast to visit her widowed sister and would not be back until late in the evening, so Velly, left to his own devices, had spent the morning catching up on some outstanding correspondence and then pottering in the garden. After lunch he decided not to waste such a fine afternoon snoozing in his armchair, but rather to go for a stroll. Accordingly he made himself presentable, picked up his favourite walking stick, locked the door and went off on one of his much-loved walks into the countryside that stretched far and wide beyond the village.

Forty minutes, and several conversations with assorted locals of his acquaintance later, he arrived at the Height, an eminence topped with ancient oaks that had a commanding view of an undulating panorama. Warmed by both the sun and the exercise, Velly sat himself down with a contented sigh on a seat that had been thoughtfully placed there in memory of some local dignitary, and prepared himself to enjoy the relaxation of a quiet sit and the pleasure of contemplating the beautiful prospect spread out before him.

After some ten minutes he was joined by a gentleman, whom he reckoned to be of about his own age, who greeted Velly with a cheery smile.

"Mind if I join you?" he enquired.

"Not at all," replied Velly, making room for the newcomer. "It's a warm sort of day for walking, isn't it?"

"Aye, when it's uphill. And I'm not as young as I was."

"Neither am I. But it's very pleasant up here. And it would be a shame not to take advantage of this beautiful weather."

"It would indeed."

There was a pause, while the newcomer made himself comfortable. Then he went on.

"Do you live here then?"

"Yes," replied Velly. "My wife and I have a cottage in the village. We've been here quite a while now. Are you from these parts too?"

"I am now. I'm from Manchester originally like, but I've knocked about a bit... I've lived in London, the North East, the Cotswolds, and now I've finally put my roots down here. At least I hope it's final – I don't want to do any more moving. I'm too old for that game now!" And he gave a merry laugh.

"No, I must admit I would not fancy moving at my time of life," said Velly. "So, how long have you been here now?"

"Three weeks since."

"Well, I'm sure you'll like it here. By the way, my name's Geddes. Velly Geddes. I should explain that Velly is short for Somervell, which sounds awfully pompous to me, so my friends have always used the shorter version."

The stranger laughed, and offered his hand to Velly.

"Put it there," he grinned. "I too have an unusual name."

"Tell me about it," urged Velly, "and about yourself."

"My family lived in Austria, where I was born," Velly's new friend began. "My parents, my two brothers and I were very happy together. We tried to live decent lives; we rarely quarrelled with anyone or made nuisances of ourselves, and we took an active part in the life of the community, but changes came, big changes that we could do nothing to prevent, changes that radically altered our life for ever. You see, we were Jews. My father was a successful music teacher, and my mother ran a little shop in our town. It always seemed to me and my brothers that nothing would ever alter our peaceful and ordered existence, but you know what happened to the Jews in the 1930s when Hitler came to power in Germany. My father decided, while there was still time, to send me to England, where fortunately we had relations in Manchester. I was only nine years old, and I was terrified. But it had to be. Otherwise I would have been 'taken away' – you know what I mean. I learned after the war that my parents, my grandparents, my brothers and my uncles and aunts had all perished at the hands of the Gestapo. I was very miserable, but my people in Manchester were very kind to me, and in the end I managed to come to some sort of terms with the sad reality of my situation. In time I was able to make something of myself. I feel English now, as much as anyone else in the country, and I shall always be grateful to the people who helped me when I was desperate."

He paused, smiled in a forced sort of way, then went on. "But we were talking about names, weren't we? I will call you Velly, if I may, and you must call be Traffy."

"With pleasure," said Velly. "But why Traffy?"

His new friend smiled, and explained.

"My family name is Kleitz. Now, when I was sent to England as a child, I went, as I said, to Manchester – to be precise, to the Trafford Park area of the city. Then after a few weeks, I was moved to another part of Manchester, to live with another aunt. My new school friends there, on learning that I had come from Trafford Park, hit on the nickname of Traffy. Now, if you connect my sobriquet Traffy with my surname, Kleitz, you have –" He stopped and threw a challenging look at Velly. "You have…?" he repeated.

"Traffy Kleitz," countered Velly, "or, if you alter the spelling a bit, traffic lights. Very clever."

They both chortled at this play on words.

"So that's why you're wearing that red, amber and green tie, I suppose?" laughed Velly.

"Quite so, though sometimes I may wear a red shirt, an orange tie, and green trousers, or some other combination," chuckled Traffy.

"Oh dear, it gets better," grinned Velly, who was both deeply moved by Traffy's story and highly amused by his whimsical sense of humour.

"Well, Traffy," said Velly, when they finally decided it was time to return to their separate homes, "I have enjoyed our little chat, and I'm pleased to have met you."

"So have I," replied Traffy. "I hope we shall meet again. I suspect we shall. I don't imagine we've solved all the world's problems this afternoon, but we've had a darned good try!"

"We'll meet again, I'm sure. You must let me know if Jessie and I can do anything for you to help you settle in here. You must visit us soon. And we'll call on you when you've had time to get organised."

"That would be a pleasure for me. I am so pleased that I have been able, for once, to talk about... things. It means so much to me. Goodbye for now, Velly."

"Goodbye, Traffy – until we next meet."

The two shook hands and parted.

Velly had been interested to hear that Traffy's father had been a professional musician. It had, so to speak, struck a chord with him, especially since to Velly himself music was a major – not to mention minor – source of pleasure. He made no claims to be possessed of any exceptional talent, but he was a cellist of no mean ability. For years he had been promising himself that when time should permit, he would dust down his cello and get down to some serious practice. He had in truth he makings of a very good player, but lack of regular and constructive practice, together with the absence of any meaningful stimulus – there being no amateur orchestra locally – had left him decidedly rusty. In fact, the only occasions upon which he played at all were when his niece came to stay. Velly greatly enjoyed these irregular sessions and, though he always complained that he was being made to work hard in order to match his niece's piano playing, he was nevertheless grateful for the sheer pleasure that music making afforded him, and for the intellectual challenge it forced him to face.

Traffy, it turned out, was a better than average pianist. Like Velly, he had allowed his skill to become slightly blunted by lack of practice and, again like Velly, he never missed the opportunity to play whenever it occurred, but he needed a more constant stimulus that would push him to improve his playing and restore it to its former high level.

One day, not long after their first meeting up on the Height, Velly and Traffy found their paths crossing again. Both had chosen this particular moment to stroll down to the Post Office to buy a morning paper. They chatted for a few moments about the weather and similar banalities before Velly brought the conversation round to the topic of music.

"Ah, there was always music in our house," Traffy told him. "My father taught the violin and the piano in our town, and he was also the cantor in the synagogue. He had a beautiful, rich voice that everyone loved to listen to. We were very proud of him. He taught me to play the piano, which I loved, and the violin, which I didn't like at all then. Mind you, I do now. Oh yes, I love to listen to the great violinists. But I have always preferred the piano, and I believe I was thought to be quite a good performer even before I left Austria. I was fortunate when I came to England because my aunt in Trafford Park had a piano and she encouraged me to play it. When I was young I was very enthusiastic, but as I grew up and as my work became a more important part of my life, I had less and less time for making music. But I hope, now that I am retired, to make good all the years of neglect. I would so love to be a good player again."

"Why shouldn't you?" asked Velly.

And, he thought, too, why shouldn't he himself become a better cellist than he was at present? Could it be that Fate had suddenly and unexpectedly thrown into his life the very stimulus he needed?

"Look here, Traffy," he went on. "We must get together to make music. I will undertake to work seriously at my cello playing, and you must do the same at your piano. We must play together. We must help each other. What do you say?"

"For my part I would welcome that. Nothing would give me more pleasure. Now we both have a purpose, a challenge."

That was how the deep friendship between the two men really began. Both freely admitted to being a bit 'rusty', and this rustiness did in fact show in the course of their first efforts together. Before long however, the old skills returned and they were soon producing very respectable sounds. Jessie, bustling in with a tray of refreshments, was both pleased and impressed. Though no musician herself, she was able to appreciate both the quality of the music making and the happiness it brought the two players. And she was delighted.

"Traffy, you must come again. Mustn't he, Velly?"

"Absolutely must. That is, if we can both stand the pace," laughed Velly. "My ageing muscles are beginning to send out early warning signals. How about you, Traffy?"

"Not really. I could play all day! It's just lack of practice. If we can meet regularly you won't suffer aches and pains."

"You must, Velly, really you must," Jessie insisted. "You've thoroughly enjoyed yourself this afternoon, haven't you?"

"I need no persuasion, and I'd be outnumbered anyway, if I did," laughed Velly. "But yes, I've had a most rewarding afternoon, and we must do this regularly."

"You've no excuse not to," Jessie pointed out reasonably. "Your time is your own, and so is Traffy's. There's no travelling involved – just a short walk for Traffy. Make it a regular date."

"As a matter of fact, I have a lot of pieces I'd like to play," replied Velly. "Of course, what we need is a violinist, and then –"

"Steady on! One thing at a time!" laughed Traffy. "But, of course, you're absolutely right. I have the Mozart Piano Trios among my music at home. I'd love to do them some time."

"Now, what about the present?" asked Jessie. "Some more music, please."

"Happy to oblige, madam. Any special little thing you'd like to request?"

"I'm happy to leave that to you," Jessie replied, making herself comfortable in her armchair.

So they played on for a while, and then concluded the session by fixing the date of their next meeting.

And that was to be just the first of many such happy occasions.

A Tragic Story

"I like that piece you were playing just now," commented Jessie, coming into the music room during a lull in the music. "It sounds very familiar – the sort of piece one hears all the time so to speak, but I can't put a name to it."

"You mean 'The Swan' of Saint-Saens," said Traffy. "It's very popular. And I think" – here he paused in a slightly dramatic way – "I may say that Velly plays it jolly well. So there."

Velly, embarrassed by such unaccustomed praise, blushed appropriately and cheerfully reciprocated Traffy's kind words. Then he became serious. He'd just been reminded of something.

"I once knew a bloke called Swann," he said, He paused, musing, then went on. "What a tragic story his was."

"I can stay for another hour or so," put in Traffy, helpfully, "If you'd like to tell us all about him."

"I hope there's going to be some more music, as well as storytelling," objected Jessie. "But if it's a good tale, I'll quickly make a pot of tea and come back and hear it." Then she added, with mock severity, "Before you resume your playing."

"Very well," agreed Velly.

When Jessie returned, Velly cleared his throat.

"This bloke Swann..." he began.

Theo Swann was a workaholic. In his early forties, he was a director of his own company, who travelled a great deal in the pursuit of advancing his business. He was often away from home for quite lengthy periods, driving himself hard and working long hours with seemingly inexhaustible energy. This naturally left him little time for any sort of home life. He had lost his first wife, Gina, when their only child, a son named Hal, was just fifteen. Hal was a rather shy, bookish lad who had applied himself assiduously to his work at school and was now, at the age of twenty, enjoying his time at Oxford.

There he had met his first and only girlfriend, Norma. Their friendship had blossomed, and it was understood to be only a question of when they would announce their engagement. Hal desperately desired Theo's approval, since he admired his father and, considering the length and frequency of Theo's absences, the two were surprisingly close. Hal was full of admiration for his father's drive, his energy, his tenacity and determination – all the positive qualities that had brought Theo, an archetypal self-made man, success in his career; but he was perhaps not quite mature or perceptive enough to see at what cost this success had been achieved, in terms of the unhappiness to which his mother had been subjected. She had been a rather introverted, very patient, giving kind of lady, anxious from the start of her married life to be unstintingly supportive of her hardworking husband, and to accept his absences as part of their married life. In time, however, she had found this neglect more and more difficult to bear, and though always putting on a cheerful face for public display, she had become increasingly unhappy as the years went by and Theo showed no sign of moderating the hectic tempo of his professional life. She never at any time breathed a word about the seething discontent that gnawed at her as mounting feelings of inadequacy and hopelessness took over her life. Hal sensed that all was not well with his mother, but he had no idea of how much she suffered in silence. Certainly it never occurred to him to attach any blame to his extraordinarily vital and successful father.

Then, soon after Hal's fifteenth birthday, on which several expensive presents arrived by post from his absent father, Gina, in a bout of depression, had been killed in a car crash. The inquest had produced a verdict of accidental death, but there was, if truth be told, more than a suggestion that Gina had deliberately driven the car off the road.

Hal had, of course, been deeply affected by his mother's

death, and when he overheard a chance reference to her suicide, supposed or actual, he was upset by both the fact itself and by its implications. The effect of this traumatic news was to make Hal more introspective. He became quiet and given to brooding, applying himself even more seriously to his studies. When later he met Norma, who was both sensitive and sensible, she had not been put off by his awkward shyness, and so by degrees he had become comfortable and relaxed in her company.

One other effect of the loss of his mother on Hal had been to increase his emotional dependence on his father. Having always admired Theo, the young man now saw in him a constant factor in his life, a source of reassurance. His mother had gone from him, but his father was still there, still someone to lean on, still someone who would support him, still there to be looked up to, to give leadership and example.

The year in question, Hal had invited Norma to spend the Easter vacation at his house. This fortunately coincided with a time when pressure of work at his office obliged Theo to be at home rather than on his travels. He had news for his son.

"Hal," he announced in his business-like way. "No beating about the bush, old son – I'm going to remarry."

The unexpected nature of this announcement deprived Hal for the moment of the power of speech. Recovering, he grinned and replied, "I say, Dad. This is a bit sudden. I mean, I'd no idea. Didn't know there was anyone... Well... You've never talked of anyone else. I mean -"

"What about 'Congratulations, Dad!' then? Or something along those lines," laughed Theo. "I presume you're pleased?"

"Of course I am, Dad. It's just that I wasn't prepared for the news. Yes, of course. Congratulations!"

"Thank you, my boy. I'm sure you'll like Freda. She's coming to stay for a few days next week. I want you and her to get to know each other and become friends. And she can meet Norma, too. After all, she will be your stepmother. I'd like to think you will be able to look upon her more as a mother."

"Tell me about her, Dad. What's she like? How did you meet her?"

"You can judge for yourself what you make of her. I can tell you that she's a fair bit younger that I am – nearer your age, in fact – that she's attractive, lively, always smartly dressed, etc., etc. Is that the sort of thing you want to know?"

"Well, yes, I suppose so. But where did you find her?"

"It was at a conference we were both attending in the autumn. I've seen quite a lot of her since, and I've liked what I've seen. We hit it off, so we're going to marry. Simple as that."

"When? Have you decided?"

"Very soon. Why have a long engagement? As soon as possible. As early as we can arrange it."

Freda duly arrived. She had driven over from town in a new bright red open-topped Jaguar. Hal had been devoting his time to his books in preparation for a forthcoming exam, using the few days prior to Norma's arrival as a time for catching up on some important revision.

Norma's arrival was planned for the 15th – two days hence – and Hal was hoping that the sudden and unexpected prior arrival of his future stepmother would not upset his plans to make Norma welcome and show her round his old childhood haunts. He was, to be honest, just a shade irritated that he and Norma would have to take second place in his father's affection. Still, he could not alter anything, and he was prepared to take things as they came. After all, he reflected, any friend of his father should be his friend too.

He was busy in the study, reading over some notes, when he heard the sound of a car pulling up on the gravel outside. He got up and crossed to the window. Looking down, he saw a smartly dressed young woman step lightly out of the car. She happened to look up as if appraising the house, and saw Hal at the study window. She flashed him a smile and gave him a little wave, having obviously guessed who he was. Slightly taken aback by her ready familiarity, Hal waved back. Then, thinking that since his father was at his office it fell to him to make Freda welcome, he opened the window and called down to tell her he was coming down. The sudden opening of the window caused several sheets of his notes to be blown off the table and fall in disarray onto the floor. Hal, briefly cursing this disruption to his work and the inconvenience of having his methodically arranged notes scattered in disorder, hurriedly left the study and went downstairs to greet the lady who was to be his stepmother.

"Hello. You must be Hal. Your father has told me all about you. I'm so pleased to meet you, Hal."

And she gave him a big hug that made him feel very awkward. Despite what his father had told him, briefly, Hal was surprised to see how youthful she was. And how attractive. He thought how clever his father was, as he always was, to have found such a woman to marry him. He could only stand there as she smilingly planted a big kiss on his cheek, and then began to see to the bits of luggage that she had brought. Hal came down to earth.

"Here, let me," he said. "I'll take those. Come on in. You must be tired after your journey. I say, I do like the car."

"Thank you," laughed Freda. "I was just beginning to wonder if you'd lost your tongue. I'm glad you like the car. Now, take me inside and show me where to put my things. Then you can show me round if you like. And I'd love a cup of tea. You know, Hal, you're taller than I'd imagined you. Mm. I think we're going to get on well together, don't you?"

She chattered on in a similar vein while Hal did his best to play the attentive host, conscious all the time that his new stepmother was doing all the running in making conversation and that he was clumsy and tongue-tied. He wished that Norma had been there to share this burden – as he saw it – of entertaining Freda. He wished above all to get back to the study to sort out his scattered notes and resume his revision. Somehow he managed to give Freda his attention until early in the evening, when Theo came home from work.

Norma's brief visit had come and gone. Theo had, to Hal's relief, taken to her and made her feel welcome under his roof, so that she and Hal were able to enjoy her stay. The only dark cloud on the horizon was that Hal sensed that Freda did not like Norma much. It was not that Freda ever said anything unkind or unfriendly – it was just an impression he had that Freda resented Norma's presence; that she was pleased to see Norma leave. Nothing however was said on either side, and Hal kept his suspicions to himself. After all, to be fair, he had to admit that similar feelings of resentment had coloured his own initial reaction to the news of Freda's coming.

A few weeks after Hal's return to Oxford, Theo and Freda were married in a quiet registry office ceremony. The reception was on a small scale, though there were several indications that wealth was behind it. Few family members were involved, but all travelled to the reception by Rolls Royce, at Theo's expense. The honeymoon took the form of a luxury cruise – not a long one, because Theo, even for such a compelling reason, was loath to let himself be kept away from his work for longer than was absolutely necessary. He already had several business trips lined up for when he and Freda returned home.

Hal had come down from university for a couple of days in order to be present at the wedding and Freda had volunteered to meet his train and convey him to the house in her car. She was visibly delighted to see Hal again and welcomed him off the train, to his great embarrassment, with a kiss and a hug, and she showed herself eager to attend to his least need. On the drive home from the station she laid her hand on Hal's knee – which, again, caused him some embarrassment – and, turning to him with a winning smile, murmured, "It's so good to see you, Hal." Then, removing her hand in order to change gear, she said, in a less confidential tone, "Your father is very pleased that you've been able to get away from your studies to be here. He thinks the world of you, you know."

Hal was not sure how best to respond, being unused to having compliments of that sort paid to him, and in so direct a fashion. He smiled weakly and remained silent, as the Jaguar, leaving the town behind, picked up speed and glided silently and powerfully along the deserted road.

"He's so proud of you. Just the way you've coped with losing your mother, sticking to your studies, getting to Oxford, and so on. And you mustn't feel embarrassed" she went on, again laying her hand on his knee, "if I too feel proud of you. I want to share in your success. I want to be a big part of your life. You will let me, won't you?" And she gave his hand a squeeze.

Hal thought that her familiarity and attentiveness were a little overdone, and he noticed that throughout the evening, she seemed to be looking at him. When Theo went upstairs to check on one or two items of his dress for the morrow, Freda smilingly came over to sit beside Hal, ostensibly to show him the ring that Theo had bought her. Hal could not help feeling that it was not absolutely necessary for her to snuggle up to him quite so closely.

"I do like that car of yours," he said. "Such a great sense of power, and so comfortable."

He made this comment in an attempt to steer the conversation away from what he suspected might be dangerous waters, and into areas where he would be more able to play a leading role in it. Once again he had the uncomfortable feeling that this woman was doing all the leading, and that he was merely following her.

"Yes," she answered. "I appreciate the power, too. And the comfort, of course. Do you drive, by the way?"

"Yes. I learned before I started at Oxford. Dad paid for me to have some lessons. I don't have a car of my own, though, and Dad's not keen to let me drive the Merc. He did sort of half-promise to buy me a car of my own after I graduate. But I've never driven anything more grand than the driving school's Fiesta."

"But you enjoy driving?"

"Oh yes. I love it."

At this point the returning Theo's footsteps were heard, and when he re-entered the room, Freda had resumed her former place in an armchair.

One of the few guests whom Freda had been responsible for inviting to the wedding was an old school chum, Anona, with whom Freda had kept in touch in adult life. Anona was a very modern young woman. Scorning marriage, she had a number of admirers in tow and enjoyed intimate relations with a string of lovers. She claimed that this arrangement kept her happy since her lovers, as she put it, "ministered to her needs" without ever being permitted to make demands upon her, either emotionally or in a practical way. She could drop any man she tired of without a twinge of conscience. The idea of being tied to one man by marrying him horrified her. Something of her attitude had rubbed off on Freda, it had to be admitted. Anona had now accepted an invitation from her old friend to spend a few days with her while Theo was away. It was some eight weeks after the wedding.

"You must get dreadfully lonely, dear," commented Anona, as they sat in the leafy garden enjoying the sunshine. "I mean, with Theo being away like this."

"I suppose so, yes." Freda paused, her eyes downcast. "Yes, to be honest I do. But Theo did sort of warn me he'd be away on business quite often. He does bring in the money, and I can't deny that I like the creature comforts that come with it."

"Such as your car," grinned Anona. "Well, anyone might envy you that. And the house," she went on, turning to gaze at the imposing façade. "It's beautiful, isn't it? You've done very well for yourself, in my opinion."

Freda looked at the house. "You know," she said, "Theo reckons the ivy on this wall is getting a bit too thick. He says it ought to be cut back and kept under control. That was his expression."

"Oh no! Let it grow. Don't restrict it."

"That's what I said. So we're leaving it and letting it grow as it pleases."

"Quite right too. I say, Freda," and she spoke in low, conspiratorial tones, "What about your stepson, Hal, eh? When I saw him at the wedding, I thought –"

"You thought what, Anona?" Freda interrupted.

"I thought, now there's a really good looking young man. I could go for him in a big way! Aren't you lucky? What's the matter, Freda? Have I said something?"

"No – it's all right." Freda had gone quiet. "You're absolutely right. He's gorgeous."

Anona giggled, but became serious as Freda went on.

"When I first met him I thought... Well... To put it simply, I fancied him. Physically, you know. That's how I felt then. And it hasn't gone away. I'm in love with him, Anona. I admit it. I want him desperately. I've said nothing to him, of course, though he may have guessed. I don't know."

"You've not said anything to Theo, of course."

"Certainly not. I'm very fond of Theo. I'm married to him, for goodness' sake. But I'm in love with Hal. Being Theo's wife means that I can see Hal whenever he comes home. Should I feel guilty, Anona? Would you, if you were in my place?"

"Certainly not! Oh, come on, Freda – join the modern world! If I were in your position I know what I'd be doing!"

"What?"

"I'd be making a put for him. I'd seduce him, and have my wicked way with him. Why don't you? He's hardly likely to tell Theo, is he? And you wouldn't. Obviously. You'd have the security of being Theo's wife, and the fun of being with Hal whenever you wanted to. Nobody need even suspect anything."

Freda needed little persuasion to convince herself that Anona was right. The fact that in confessing to Anona her feelings toward Hal she had spoken out loud of her love served only to reinforce that love in her mind. It also intensified her need to gratify her desire, while at the same time blinding her to the damage and distress that would be caused if Theo were ever to find out. Hal's diffidence and lack of experience in what Anona lightly referred to as the modern world might prove to be obstacles, but Freda did not doubt that she would be able to overcome them. It never occurred to her that Hal might be disgusted by her advances because of his love for, and loyalty to, Norma.

Anona left a few days later on a hot sunny morning. Her parting words, as she drove off were, "Best of luck with you know what".

Freda watched the car disappear up the road, then turned and walked slowly back towards the house. Maybe Theo is right about the ivy, she thought, letting her gaze run along the façade. Perhaps it does need trimming, or it will run out of control. But it's too hot to worry about it just now. She sat down, on the same garden seat that she had used before when making her confession to Anona. She thought over what she had told her friend, and also Anona's reaction. But it's so easy for her, thought Freda. She has no ties; she's free. Furthermore, she has no conscience. A prey to conflicting emotions, Freda leaned back, and closed her eyes. Before long she fell asleep in the warm sunshine, serenaded by the song of the birds in her beautiful, peaceful garden. She awoke half an hour later with a headache. She went indoors, took an aspirin and went to lie down.

She resolved now to look on Hal as only a son. She would not cheat on Theo. Anona was Anona – she moved in a different world.

The next day dawned hot and sunny once again. Freda awoke to find her headache had gone, and she felt refreshed and invigorated. She promised herself that she would keep away from the sun as much as possible. And keep away from the son too, she mused, allowing herself a faint smile at the pun. She thought briefly of Hal, but it was only to tell herself that he was too busy at Oxford, some seventy miles away, and she managed more or less to put him out of her mind. The morning's drowsy heat continued throughout the day, and Freda was glad to stay indoors, quietly reading by an open window, or strolling outside around the shady areas of the garden.

The weather remained hot as the following day dawned, and the sun streamed in through a gap in the curtains, promising another perfect summer's day. When the post arrived there were several letters for Theo, all connected as usual with his business interests, Freda surmised. There was also one letter for her. It was a brief note from Anona, thanking her for making her short visit such an enjoyable one and informing Freda that one of Anona's beaux was taking her away for a short break in a few days' time. The brief note ended with a shameless query as to how things were progressing between her and Hal. Freda put the letter down and sighed. She suddenly felt lonely again. She resented Theo's long and frequent absences; they made her feel unwanted, and that wasn't fair.

She thought of Hal. But he would be on his way to stay with Norma and her parents as the next day was Norma's birthday and a small party had been planned. Perhaps Hal and Norma intended to use the occasion to announce their engagement? Freda shivered without understanding why, and felt a surge of resentment against Norma. He'll have no time for me, she told herself bitterly, any more than his father does when he's away. Suddenly she longed to see Hal, to have him near her, to touch him, to put her arms round him, to hold him close to her in an embrace that was not a motherly one. Freda tried in vain to push these thoughts aside.

The room darkened suddenly as a cloud passed over the sun. Freda got up, crossed to the window and looked up at the sky. Gone now was the clear, unbroken blue of the earlier past of the day; an eerie orange grey, lowering and ominous, covered all the sky that she could see. It felt stuffy in the room. Freda threw open the French windows, yet this brought no welcome coolness. It was as airless outside as indoors. Rumbles of thunder broke the silence faintly in the distance. Everything was still, and an uncomfortable heaviness hung in the atmosphere. Not a leaf stirred and, apart from the thunder, there was no sound. Freda stood by the open French windows, looking up at the sky and feeling uneasy in the sticky, oppressive heat. She was aware of being alone, slightly frightened, vulnerable and frustrated.

As she stood there, an unfamiliar car pulled up outside. Freda, who was not expecting any visitors, was amazed and more than a little disconcerted to see Hal get out and walk towards her.

"Hal," she said quietly. "This is a pleasant surprise. I wasn't expecting you. I thought you were on your way to see Norma."

"I had planned originally to leave Oxford tomorrow and do the journey in one go," Hal explained. "But since there were one or two things I wanted to pick up from here, I thought I'd set off today, spend the night here and then go on to Lincolnshire tomorrow. It's no trouble, as I've hardly had to go out of my way at all to come here."

A loud clap of thunder rent the air, just as, with a strange wailing sound, a brisk, gusty wind began to blow, causing the big heavy curtains to billow out and sending Anona's note fluttering to the floor. Then the rain began to fall in torrents. Hal hurried to close the French windows. At exactly the same moment Freda moved to pick up Anona's letter, and in doing so bumped into Hal. Unable to stop herself, Freda pulled Hal to her and kissed him on the lips.

"Hal, oh Hal," she murmured urgently. "It's so good to see you again. I'm missing your father so much. I'm so alone. You see that, don't you? Kiss me, Hal. Be nice to me. You love me, don't you?"

She did not wait for him to answer, but went on. "Let me get you something to drink. You must be very thirsty. It's such thirsty weather, isn't it? I'll have something too. Here, sit down. What would you like?"

"I'd like a long cool glass of beer more than anything else," Hal replied, taken aback by the warmth and urgency of the welcome he'd received.

He flopped into an armchair, loosened his collar and stretched his limbs.

Freda meanwhile, as she fetched the drinks, was in a state of mental turmoil. Why, on the same day that Anona's letter had arrived, had it been followed so soon afterwards by Hal's turning up out of the blue? Was it a simple coincidence, or was fate playing some cruel game with her? All she knew for certain was that Hal was back with her, and she wanted him more than ever. Fate had also arranged for Theo to be away; was that mere coincidence? Freda saw that she must waste no time, since Hal was only stopping overnight then moving on next morning. How could she detain him? An idea occurred to her – a crude, banal idea born of desperation.

It was a superb storm. The thunderclaps rumbled on with hardly a break, while lightning flashed at ever-shortening intervals and the rain continued to lash against the windowpanes as the wind kept up its eerie howling. The heat grew stifling. Freda brought Hal and herself one drink, then another, then another. Snuggling up to him, she used the excuse of the heat to unfasten and remove her blouse, and then did the same with Hal's shirt. Hal, in a daze, reeling from the effects of the unaccustomed consumption of so much alcohol and only half aware of what he was doing, allowed himself to be led by Freda into her bedroom. Soon they were both naked on the bed.

As soon as she was quite sure that Hal was fast asleep, Freda, who held her drink better than her stepson, rose from the bed and, quickly slipping on some clothes, quietly removed the key of Hal's hired car from his trouser pocket and went downstairs. The hired car stood on the drive where Hal had left it. Having opened the bonnet, she proceeded methodically to carry out a plan to make Hal stay by ensuring that his car would not start. Having carried out this mission, she replaced the key and went back to bed.

Hal woke the next morning, wondering at first where he was; he had never slept in his parents' bedroom before. He also had a bad headache and that reminded him of what had happened the previous evening. Freda was already up and preparing breakfast. After his head slowly cleared an awful awareness of what he had done came to Hal. He was supposed to be going to the house of the girl he loved, the girl he intended to marry, yet here he was, in a half-dazed state in his stepmother's bed. He had to get away from her as quickly as possible. He must be on the road with the least possible delay, and he must hope that, please God, Norma would never find out what he had done. Nor must his father find out. Hell, what a mess! How had it happened? He remembered the storm, the stifling heat, the drink. God, what a mess! Dragging himself out of bed and into awareness, he took a cold shower which helped, and went downstairs to get some breakfast.

Freda gave him a smile and went to embrace him as he entered the kitchen, but he pushed her away angrily.

"Why do you do this?" he demanded. "Why? Why?"

Freda remained unmoved by his anger. She told him, with a coolness that maddened him, that it was as much his doing as hers. If he couldn't take his drink, well, it was hardly her fault.

"Anyway," she concluded. "Whatever you may think or say, I certainly am not sorry, so don't expect any apologies from me. Now, have something to eat, and you can be on your way. And when you've eaten," she added, "Take a couple of aspirins. Here."

As if in a dream, Hal forced some food down his throat, and drank some coffee that Freda smilingly poured for him. Then, scarcely deigning to say goodbye, he walked out to the car. Freda watched as he attempted to start the engine. Of course, nothing happened. After some ten minutes Hal, who knew nothing about car engines, admitted defeat.

"I can't get the damned thing to start," he muttered angrily. "This is a hell of a nuisance."

Freda stood with her arms folded, leaning against the doorway, watching him, unable to stop a half-smile.

In a Lincolnshire village some thirty miles away, a young woman had been receiving cards, presents and congratulations from her family. The high point of her twentieth birthday celebrations was however to come that evening, when a small gathering of friends, neighbours and relations would join in wishing Norma well, to drink her health and generally enjoy themselves in informal style. For Norma, the highlight of the day would be the moment when Hal would slip a ring on her finger and they would publicly announce their engagement. Hal was speeding on his way to her now and would soon be with her she thought, happily anticipating his arrival.

Freda's plan appeared to be working; it looked as if Hal would have to postpone his departure to visit Norma until a mechanic could be sent for and the car attended to. Hal even feared that if the trouble turned out to be serious he might have to put off his visit altogether; after all, if he couldn't be there for the party on the day itself, anything else would be something of an anti-climax. No, he had to get there today. But how?

Freda, watching him, saw his gaze turn to the garage where her Jaguar stood. He turned and walked slowly towards her.

"Look," he began awkwardly, and with obvious embarrassment. "I'm sorry I was a bit short with you just now. And I admit that what happened was as much... Well, I'm as much to blame as you. It was because of the drink. I'm just not used to it. And the heat, and everything". He paused, then "Look, I don't suppose..." And he looked towards the Jaguar.

Freda felt a wave of sympathy sweep over her. He looked so pathetic, so helpless. She felt genuinely sorry for him. True, his mission was to get to the girl he really loved, but she admitted to herself that she had treated him, in the circumstances, very badly; she'd been selfish, she'd used him. It was the sort of thing Anona might do, and have no qualms about it, but, poor lad... She felt she owed him something for the way she had treated him. She laid her hand on his arm.

"Give me a minute or two to change," she told him. "We'll go in the Jag."

She added as an afterthought as she re-entered the house, "You can drive. You'd like that, I know. And I can drive myself back."

She was back with him in ten minutes and, after locking the house, she handed him the keys of her car.

"Just be careful," she said. "This car isn't quite the same as the one you came in. There's a lot of power under that bonnet, and," she added, "the roads will probably still be a bit wet after all the rain."

Theo was a bit surprised when he returned home late that same afternoon, to find the house empty. He wondered what the strange car was doing that was parked on the drive. He knew that Hal would be away, but had expected to find Freda at home, since she had told him that she would not be going to Norma's party. Perhaps she'd changed her mind? Then he discovered that the Jaguar was not in the garage. Yes, she must have changed her mind and gone with Hal after all. Theo was pleased, if indeed this was the case. He decided that he might as well follow them, and accordingly set off immediately for Lincolnshire.

Freda had been right; the roads were wet and greasy. The Jaguar, however, handled well. Hal felt in control, as he did not often feel in Freda's company. He smiled to himself, wallowing in the exhilarating comfort of the driving-seat, as his hands caressed the steering wheel. He forgot that it was Freda who was sitting beside him, and imagined it was Norma. He and Norma would own a car like this. He pressed the accelerator gently, and the car responded with a surge of speed. He slowed down for a bend. Yes, this was the sort of car to have. He'd learnt to drive in a small one, and the one he'd hired had no real power. But the Jag had everything – comfort, ease, luxury and power. Hal wondered what his father intended to buy for him when he reached his twenty first birthday. He pressed the accelerator again and the car leaped forwards, like a panther springing. A panther, or a jaguar. What other cars were like this, could compare with this? There were other makes, of course. His father's Mercedes was a beautiful machine. There were BMWs, Lotuses, etc. Hal made a mental note of all the various models he and Norma would look at, would test drive when -
    "Look out!"
    Freda's anguished scream dragged Hal out of his daydream. But she was too late. Hal had to swerve violently to

avoid a small child who suddenly ran out from behind a hedge, and the car skidded on the damp greasy surface. The Jaguar left the road, careered out of control onto the grass verge and smacked head-on into a very solid, unyielding tree at eighty miles an hour. Hal and Freda were both killed instantly, and the car was a complete write-off.

The bodies had been removed, but the remains of the Jaguar were still there when the unsuspecting Theo Swann arrived at the spot.

A shocked silence greeted the termination of Velly's story. Then Jessie said, "That was terrible. Terrible. Those poor young people."

Traffy went over to the piano and, without saying a word, began to play the Funeral March from Chopin's Op. 35 sonata.

Reasons for Reasons

One morning Traffy was improvising in a leisurely way at the piano while Velly was looking through a pile of music. Jessie came in with a tray of coffee and biscuits.

"What are you playing today?" she asked. "Something bright and cheerful, I hope."

"It all depends," replied Velly, "on whether or not I can find what I'm searching for. I thought it was in this pile, but I've been right through it, and it's not there."

"What is it you're after?" enquired Traffy, emerging from his private world as Velly attacked another sheaf of music that he'd just unearthed from the drawer of the cabinet.

"I thought it would be a nice idea to tackle the-ah! Got it! It was here all the time."

Velly rose triumphantly from his knees and tidied away the music he had been looking through. "I can't imagine why it was there, among these sonatas. I must have put it there ages ago, for some strange reason."

"There's always a reason for everything, dear," said Jessie.

"And reasons for reasons," countered Velly. "This reminds me of the story of the little girl who arrived late for a dental appointment because some child was fractious in a supermarket."

"I don't see the connection," objected Jessie.

"That's the point," Velly explained. "It's all because X then Y, and because Y then Z. One thing leads to another, and the chain can go on and on, as long as you like."

"That's true," Traffy put in. "Consider, for example, Bill and Sue."

"Who, for goodness' sake, are Bill and Sue?" enquired Velly. "And what have they got to do with anything?"

"Bill and Sue Hicks were a couple my wife and I got to know when we were first married. We were living in the Midlands at the time. We became quite friendly with them, even though they were a fair bit older than we were. One day they told us about how they first met. Not just how, but why. As Jessie was saying just now, there's a reason for everything and -"

"And reasons for reasons," quipped Velly, for the second time.

"Do tell us about this couple," begged the practical Jessie. But don't let your coffee go cold."

*

"Bill had lost his father while still a child," Traffy began, "and he was brought up by his mother. He was quite musical – singing was his main interest, and as a young man he joined a local choir. It was through this choir that he first met Sue, whom he eventually married. But there are several threads to this story. Let me tell you all of them, and you'll see how they all come together."

"Reasons f-"

"Exactly, Velly."

The tale begins in the town of Hasterleigh where, quite by chance, the local branch of the Mayfair National Bank came to be short-staffed as a result of a sudden resignation and a couple of cases of long-term illness. So Sue Marlow was drafted in from another branch twenty miles away to fill in for as long as might prove to be necessary. Sue was in her twenties, was a dedicated employee, and had been with the bank long enough to be well acquainted with its working practices. That clearly was why she had been chosen to go to Hasterleigh.

Sue was fortunate enough to find a nice little bedsit in the Crawford Road near the church, and soon settled in. Now, being the possessor of a pleasant contralto voice, she wished to find a local choir to join, as much for social as for musical reasons. Her landlady, Mrs Gill, a comfortable and friendly body who had been widowed several years previously, agreed that joining a choir was as good a way as any of meeting people and making new friends. Fortunately she knew Mr. Wells, who was the conductor of the Hasterleigh Singers, and was therefore able to inform Sue that the choir met for practice each Tuesday evening at the Church Hall, which was only a hundred yards away up the Crawford Road. Sue thanked Mrs. Gill and decided that she would go along to the practice and join the Hasterleigh Singers the following week.

Tom, the caretaker of the Church Hall, had just finished fitting a new lock to the main door. Gathering together his tools, he locked the hall and returned home for his lunch. His wife met him as he walked in, an anxious expression on her face and anxiety and agitation showing in her demeanour.

"What's up?" enquired Tom, seeing that all was not well.

"It's mum," she replied. "I've just had her neighbour on the phone. Mum's had a stroke. She's in a bad way. I'll have to go to her. She's been taken to the hospital."

"I'll drive you over, lass," Tom said, laying a reassuring hand on her arm. "Do you want to go straight away? Lunch can wait. We can get something to eat there. We can be at the hospital in two hours."

"That's good of you, dear. Yes, I would like to go straight away. I can't bear to think of her lying there, all alone. You don't mind, do you?"

"Of course not. Come on. Get your things together and we'll be off."

They were halfway to their destination when Tom suddenly realised that he still had in his jacket pocket the keys to the new locks he had fitted, and he was immediately aware that nobody would be able to unlock the hall for the Hasterleigh Singers practice that evening. He said nothing to his wife, but consoled himself with the fact that they would possibly be able to return to Hasterleigh in time anyway. There was no need to panic, but Tom decided that it would be sensible to inform the vicar as soon as he could.

The vicar was, naturally, most sympathetic when his caretaker phoned to say that his mother-in-law was poorly, and he fully appreciated that it was necessary, in the circumstances, for Tom and his wife, who didn't drive, to stay overnight near the hospital, rather than return to Hasterleigh that afternoon. He told Tom not to worry about the problem of the key to the hall.

"You have more important things to worry about," he said. "If your mother-in-law is in such a bad state, of course you must stay, so that your wife can be at her mother's side. Now, I shall telephone Mr Wells and explain the situation to him. Tonight's practice will just have to be cancelled, that's all there is to it. I'm quite sure Mr Wells will understand. Now, don't worry. Everything will be all right this end."

Bill Hicks' mother was in her late fifties and, perhaps partly because she had borne single-handedly the burden of bringing up two sons, was becoming a trifle absent-minded. It wasn't a problem as such, and she and her sons would laugh about it, while she accepted their good-natured teasing in the spirit in which it was meant. They were both very fond of their mother.

On the Tuesday afternoon in question, Mr Wells had telephoned while Bill and his brother were both still at work. Mrs Hicks had just opened her front door prior to going out to do some late afternoon shopping, when the phone rang. Mr. Wells was contacting as many choir members as he could, in time to inform them of the cancellation of that evening's practice. Mrs Hicks assured him that she would tell Bill as soon as he got in from work. She would certainly be back from her shopping trip by then. It was unfortunate that she did not make a note of Mr Wells' message, trusting instead to her memory and assuming that she would, in any case, see Bill later, as usual.

Bill's brother Howard was a motorcycling enthusiast, and he spent many hours happily tinkering with his two machines. He was the proud owner of an aged BSA and an up-to-date Japanese model, and would jokingly refer to them collectively as his 'hymn book, Ancient and Modern'. He subscribed to a magazine for people such as himself, and had a large pile of past copies of the publication in his bedroom. Having read all of them from cover to cover, he decided he had no more need of them all, and had set aside a pile that he intended to throw out. It happened, however, that Bill had been chatting to a colleague at work who, like Howard, was mad on motorbikes. When Bill mentioned that Howard was planning to dispose of a large pile of magazines devoted to motorcycling, his colleague had immediately expressed an interest.

"Don't let him just throw them out. I'd love to have a look at them, if you're sure he's finished with them."

"Oh, definitely. Look, I'll bring them round to your house tonight, if you like. It's no trouble. I'm going to choir-practice tonight, so I can easily call at your place afterwards and give them to you then, if that's okay."

"Hang on. That might be awkward. Jean and I are going out tonight, so there'll be nobody in. Hmm. Unless you called in earlier – we shan't be leaving till about half seven."

"No problem. I'll call in on my way to the practice. I'll just set off a bit earlier than usual, that's all."

"Great. See you tonight, then. And thanks."

Having received the vicar's phone-call, in which he explained why the choir practice had had to be cancelled, Mr Wells the choirmaster made some more calls himself, contacting various members of the choir, who in turn undertook to pass the message on to others. The last person Mr Wells contacted was Jeff, one of the basses.

"Has Bill Hicks been informed?" Jeff asked him.

"Oh yes. I think everybody knows now. I didn't actually speak to Bill, but I left a message with his mother. So he'll know."

"There's no need for me to phone him then."

"Oh no. I'll see you next week, all being well."

Bill's mother had just finished her shopping at the supermarket and was wheeling her trolley out to where her car was parked.

To her dismay, she found that one of the car's tyres was flat. On investigation, she found a large nail embedded in it. Luckily, a young man in a sports car realised her predicament and gallantly offered to change the wheel for her. He took control of the situation in a very business-like way, much to Mrs. Hicks's relief. He found the jack and soon had the wheel with the flat tyre removed. But when he came to fit the spare wheel his jaunty air changed to one of concern.

"This tyre is very bald," he told Mrs. Hicks. "In fact, it's not legal. See, the tread is completely worn here… and here… and here."

"Oh dear. What should I do?" she asked, feeling very helpless.

He thought for a moment.

"Look," he said, "I'll put the spare on, with the worn tyre, but it must be only a temporary measure and you must get rid of that tyre as soon as you possibly can. My advice to you would be to go straight to the Hasterleigh Tyre Co's place, just up the road there" – and he pointed it out – "and get them to put a new tyre on this wheel. They can be repairing the puncture at the same time."

Mrs Hicks could see the sense of this. There was no sense in taking a risk with a bald tyre. She blamed herself for not having a proper spare.

But one can't remember everything.

And it was while she was waiting at the Hasterleigh Tyre Co to have the tyres seen to that she remembered Mr Wells' phone call. She hoped, however, that she would still be able to get home before Bill set off for his evening out.

"Mum's late tonight," said Howard. "No doubt she's found one of her friends and they're having a good natter."

"Who knows?" replied Bill. "By the way, which magazines -"

"Ah yes. It's this pile here. Your mate is very welcome to them, and you can tell him I don't want them back. You're off now, are you? Bit early?"

"Yes, but it's because I'm delivering these magazines before choir, not afterwards. It's a bit of a detour, so I'm leaving a good twenty minutes early. I don't suppose mum'll be long now. It's not the first time, after all. Anyway, I must be off. See you later."

"Cheerio. Have a good sing."

"I'm sure I shall."

Bill was surprised, on arriving at the Church Hall, to find it deserted. He usually expected to see several other cars in the car park belonging to other choir members who had arrived before him. Mr Wells especially was always there in good time, so the absence of his car particularly puzzled Bill. He parked his car and walked over to the door of the hall. It was, of course, locked. Bill decided to wait for a while in his car to see if anyone else turned up. He looked at his watch. The usual time. Where was everybody? Glancing round, he noticed an attractive young lady walking over. He wound down the window.

"Excuse me," she said. "I don't know if I've come to the right place. Is this where the Hasterleigh Singers meet? Have I got the day right?"

"Yes, and yes," Bill assured her. "I don't understand why no one else is here. Are you planning to join us then?"

"Yes. That is, if you'll have me. I sing contralto."

"Then you'll be very welcome indeed. By the way, I'm Bill Hicks. I sing in the tenors."

"I'm Sue Marlow. Pleased to meet you."

They waited another twenty minutes or so, while Bill told Sue something about the choir, its repertoire, personnel, concerts, etc.

Then Sue said, "Would you like to come round to my flat and telephone the choirmaster, or secretary, or somebody, from there? Then at least we'll know what's going on. I only live just up the road."

"That sounds like a sensible idea," Bill replied.

"And that," concluded Traffy, "was how Bill met Sue. But you see how easily it could never have happened, how everything depended upon chance."

"Very clever," said Jessie. "It's almost like something out of Thomas Hardy, but with a happy ending."

"There's probably a reason for every coincidence, if only we knew it," mused Traffy. "But," and he became more decisive, "Some music! What shall we play? What about that piece you were hunting for just now, Velly?"

"What is this piece anyway?" Jessie wanted to know.

"Oh yes. It's actually a rather pleasant arrangement for cello and piano of one of Ivor Novello's songs."

"Which one?" asked Jessie enthusiastically. "I do so love his music."

"Love is my reason," replied Velly, with a broad smile.

"As I said just now," commented Traffy, "There's always a reason."

Two Brothers

"I hope I've come to the right house," the stranger began. "It sounds very quiet just now – ominously quiet, you might say – but I was assured that this was the house."

He was a tall, lean man, casually dressed, probably in his early sixties, and he had a mischievous twinkle in his eye. Nevertheless, his reason for being there, on the front doorstep of Velly's house left poor Velly, who had opened the door in response to the knock, completely nonplussed.

"I'm sorry," he began, looking the stranger up and down, and rather liking what he saw, despite his bewilderment at the newcomer's words. "I don't follow you. Why this house, my house?"

"The house of music?" the man suggested. "Is this not the house where music is played? I gather that at certain times on certain days the wondrous sounds of cello and piano in glorious harmony may be heard, and I wondered whether perhaps…"

"Come in, come in," said Velly, "and tell me what all this is about." Velly was intrigued.

He settled the stranger in a comfortable armchair and addressed him.

"It is true that my friend and I meet fairly regularly to play chamber music. I'm a cellist of sorts, and my friend, who lives just round the corner, is a pianist of a better sort. We make music in our limited way because we love it and because it gives us so much pleasure. We are, as I said, limited, because there are only the two of us. We really need a decent violinist, you see, and then -"

The stranger held up his hand.

"Dare I?" he asked. "Dare I ask you to consider admitting me to your privileged circle? I have played the violin for more years than I care to remember, and I wish to continue to do so."

Velly's face lit up. Was it possible that here sat the very person whom he and Traffy had been missing? Here was a violinist, the violinist, who would enable them to play trios.

"The Mozart Piano Trios," he sighed, with a smile.

"I beg your pardon?"

"Oh, it's simply that Traffy and I have dreamed about playing the Mozart Trios, but we needed a violinist. Then, suddenly, out of the blue, you turn up. Tell me frankly – how good a player are you? Oh, I say, that sounds awfully rude. What I mean is, suppose we – that is , you – were to -"

"Not at all," he laughed. "Well, it's hardly for me to say, is it? I played regularly with the Burnside Orchestra in the firsts until about six months ago, so I'm not altogether rusty."

"My word," said Velly, impressed. Burnside was some forty miles away, and Velly had heard glowing reports of the quality of the orchestra there.

"My wife died two years ago," the man went on, "and so I lived alone for a while, more or less looking after myself. But when my son and his wife came to live here, we bought between us a house that was big enough for me to have a little flat of my own there. So I'm still to a large extent independent, though my son and daughter-in-law are there on the spot if I need them."

"You look as if you're the sort of bloke who can look after himself," said Velly.

"Oh, I keep fit. And I practise the violin daily. By the way, my name is Dunyan. Rhymes with Bunyan, as in *Pilgrim's Progress*. My first name is John, also like Bunyan's."

"Well, it seems that your pilgrimage has brought you to the right place," Velly reassured him, finally introducing both himself and Jessie, who had just returned from the village shop. "Look, John, be here tomorrow morning at ten, with your violin. It'll give Traffy a nice little surprise to meet you, and we'll see how we get on."

John Dunyan arrived promptly at Velly's house the following

morning, prepared for a session of music making. Traffy was already there and, as Velly had foreseen, was delighted to find that they now had a violinist in their company. Velly explained to John, to his great amusement, how Traffy had come by his nickname. Traffy, not to be outdone, caused more mirth when he declared that anyone with the surname Dunyan would have to be called Pickle. So Pickle it was from then on. Pickle himself was delighted; it made him feel, even before he had played a note, that he belonged to the group. His cheerful good humour and lurking sense of fun proved invaluable assets, and when Velly thought back to the recent past, before he had met either Traffy or Pickle, he could hardly believe his good fortune. Jessie, too, was delighted with the way things had gone.

"What are you three unwise monkeys playing today?" she enquired one morning, several weeks after Pickle had joined them.

"There's still that last Mozart trio we haven't looked at yet," replied Traffy. "And I have been practising it in secret. Shall we give it a go?"

"I'm ready," said Velly. "Okay, Pickle?"

"Okay by me, Give us an A, will you, Traffy?"

The music was on the stands, and the two stringed instruments were tuned to the piano.

They were about to begin playing when Pickle said, quite out of the blue, "I was reading a curious legend yesterday, about a violin player."

"Keep it for the coffee-break," decreed Velly. "Then Jessie can hear it too." How could he have sensed that there was a story here in the offing? "We love storytelling by the way, and we can often find the odd story connected with the music we're playing."

"Oh, this has nothing to do with Mozart, but I thought it was a good story. Anyway, I'll keep it for later. Meanwhile, let's get back to Mozart. I'll count three, then we're all in together. A good, firm start; and let's hear Traffy's little run up to the first chord."

And they were off. Velly was secretly quite pleased that

Pickle had a domineering streak in him; it was just what a small chamber group needed in its leader. Not that he was at all overbearing – just firm enough to give a positive lead and hold things together. Things were looking up. As for Traffy, the happy smile on his face as he played was evidence enough that he relished the extra dimension that a good violinist gave them.

"Ah, teamwork," he murmured, as if to himself, as they brought the first movement to a close.

Jessie came in with a tray of refreshments just at the right moment, and needed no persuading to stay and listen to Pickle's story.

"It's an old Breton legend," Pickle began. "I found it in an antiquated volume of folk tales from France that I picked up at the weekend at the Antiques Fair in Middlehurst. You have to believe in fairies and goblins and such if you're to make anything of this tale. In this case, the supernatural element is provided by a species of little people called the Korrigans, who were apparently generally feared by the superstitious folks of Brittany because they could be very unfriendly toward humans, though it turns out they weren't always malevolent. It seems to me, also, that they knew a thing or two about justice – at least on the evidence of this little narrative. Anyhow, cast your minds back a few centuries, and I'll tell you the story of two brothers."

Gaspard and Yann were brothers, but they could hardly have been more different. Gaspard, a tall, powerful young man in his late twenties, had an air of confident, not to say arrogant, self-assurance about him; a hint of a complacent smile seemed always to play around his thin lips, and his upright bearing and swaggering manner were suggestive of one who was accustomed to have his own way and would not be patient toward anyone who might attempt to thwart him. Yet the smile was not a happy one, and he never gave the impression of being contented with his lot. No, he was a scheming, selfish, impatient fellow, quick to find fault and equally quick to lose his temper. Then the sly smile would give way to an ugly scowl, and the handsome face would cloud over, to mock the vigorous, upright body by casting, as it were, a cloak of ugliness over his entire person. All too often his ill-natured side would seek to assert itself at the expense of Yann, who was two years his junior. Where Fate had seemingly favoured Gaspard in his physical development, she had clearly seen in Yann an excuse to exercise her talent for mischief, for Yann was cursed with an ugly hump on his back that obliged him to walk with an ungainly stoop. No sympathy for his brother's misfortune ever passed Gaspard's lips; indeed, he preferred to mock his younger brother, and to find in him a source of cruel laughter, as if the suffering of another fellow-creature served to increase his awareness of himself as a superior being. Yann, however, bore all the taunts and jeers directed at him with the patience of a saint. Only when he was finally completely alone in his bed at the end of the day's work did he think back on the unpleasant jibes of his brother, to wonder why things were as they were, and whether they would always be so. But never, never, did any thought that some day, in some way, he might take his revenge ever come to him. By contrast with Gaspard, Yann was always the most cheerful of men. Those who knew them both used to say that the personalities of the brothers had, surely, by some curious chance, been allocated wrongly by Fate. They could, they used to say, have understood Gaspard, with all the gifts that Nature had bestowed on him, being the happiest and most easy-going of men. Likewise, it would have been understandable if Yann, cursed as he was from birth, had been of a sour and gloomy disposition. The reverse however was the case, and the fact remained that, whereas Gaspard was not popular in the village, Yann was well liked. Many a young maiden, on first setting eyes on Gaspard, had been attracted to him by his good looks, but had decided, on better acquaintance, that she had no wish to link her destiny with his. Yann, for his part, took it for granted that no girl would ever give him a second glance, on account of the repulsive hump he carried on his back.

The brothers lived alone in a cottage not far from the seashore. Their father, a fisherman, had drowned in his boat during a violent storm at sea some six years previously, having brought up his two sons on his own since his wife had died in giving birth to Yann. When the boys were orphaned, the villagers rallied round to give them support and practical help, until they were able to stand on their own feet. One or two of them wondered whether Gaspard's treatment of his unfortunate brother, of which everybody in the village and the fishing community was aware, was perhaps due to his seeing Yann as a burden. If Gaspard did in fact imagine this he certainly had no cause to, for Yann never shirked doing his share of the work, preparing the meals, repairing the nets, maintaining their boat, and looking after their little garden.

Fate had however, in one respect, given Yann a trump card. As if she had reasoned that the poor fellow deserved some kind of compensation, some positive gift to offset his disadvantage, she had given him the priceless gift of music. Yann was a very talented fiddler, and no wedding or feast or festival passed in the village without Yann's being invited to provide the music for the guests to dance to. On these occasions he became a person of some importance; everyone acknowledged his talent and praised his skill with the bow. Indeed, they used to say that when Yann played there was no resisting the urge to get up and dance. There were also those who said that his bow had magic qualities.

Around the time of his twentieth birthday, Yann had been to attend the festivities at the Vieux Manoir, the stately home of Maitre Queguirec. Maitre Queguirec was a wealthy lawyer, whose wife had borne him a son and two daughters, and the cause of the celebrations was the success of the son, who had just returned from his studies in far-off Paris and who was now to become, like his father, a lawyer. Never was a man more proud of his son than Maitre Queguirec! And never was a man so ready to celebrate in such lavish style, for he was a generous, hearty man, whom business had not hardened, but rather mellowed. He loved good cheer and jollity, and to see other people happy was all he asked. His heart would go out to those he had to disappoint when they came to him for advice and help, and many a time he would waive his fee if he saw hardship lying beyond the paying of it, though he never had scruples over making his wealthy clients pay, particularly those whose prosperity he suspected had not been earnt in completely honest dealings. This then, was the man who was sparing no expense in order to ensure a fitting welcome home for his beloved son. The celebrations must, of course, include dancing on the spacious lawns of the Manoir, and who better than Yann to provide the music?

Maitre Queguirec's two beautiful daughters and their mother did all in their power to ensure that the festivities passed off as well as could be hoped, and that all who attended would never forget the evening's merry-making. The eldest daughter Marie, with her sweetheart Paul always at her side, was most attentive in seeing to it that the guests never lacked food or drink. Maitre Queguirec, with his wife on his arm, circulated amongst the revellers, chatting with everyone, having a friendly word and a merry quip for servant and master alike. Her sister Annette, a quiet and modest beauty in her twentieth year, preferred to stay in the shadow of her adored brother. Annette admired him not merely in the manner of a dutiful younger sister but also, and chiefly because he had worked hard for something and had attained it. In her eyes, this set him apart from the various young men she had met in her young life, men about whom she could not entertain serious thoughts because as she saw it, whatever they possessed was inherited or bought rather than gained by effort and merit. There was nothing that they did particularly well; how could she look up to such as them? Still Annette, for all her retiring demeanour, drew admiring looks from several young men that night.

Among these admirers was one who, seeing Annette for the first time, was bowled over by not only her beauty but also by the sweetness of her expression, the modesty of her bearing, the friendliness of the smile that she gave to each person to whom she spoke. This, the young man reflected, was the daughter of the great and wealthy Maitre Queguirec; yet she was no haughty, condescending, arrogant beauty acting the proud lady and patronising the humble locals. She was, he mused as he gazed at her, not only... But the young man had a job to do making music, and the lady herself was endeavouring, like her brother, to find time to exchange words with all the guests, if that were possible. So she passed on, having smiled shyly at Yann and thanked him for the beauty and the warmth of his playing. She told him she admired his skill, and would have said more, but was led away by her brother to join the dancers. Yann watched her go, coaxing a soulful melody, full of longing and sadness, out of his violin. He was, after all, a man and susceptible to the attractions of the opposite sex, even though he had long since schooled himself to accept that no woman would ever fall in love with him. In this awareness of his inferiority to his fellows he had, of course, been generously aided by his brother.

Yann thought longingly of Annette and, in the privacy of his little room, asked God why he had been created so ugly. Then, as always, he sought consolation in his mastery of his trusty violin.

But he could not forget Annette.

Two years had passed, and once again Maitre Queguirec was hosting a lavish celebration at the Manoir. This time the occasion was the wedding of his daughter Marie. Once again, Yann was, naturally, called upon to provide the music for the dancing. The occasion was no less splendid a gathering than had been the festivities with which the wealthy lawyer had honoured Marie's brother. Annette was there by her sister's side, an efficient and attentive bridesmaid. Again, Yann was captivated by her. Again, as before, she came and spoke to him, telling him shyly how much she admired his playing. Yann tried to deceive himself into thinking that he detected a touch of extra warmth in her manner toward him, but he dismissed the thought. If it were true, he told himself, it is because of her generous nature and not because she can have any feelings for me. So he dismissed from his mind the idea that this girl could ever be anything more to him than any other girl he might meet. It made her seem all the more unattainable to him, and made him love her all the more. Annette, for her part, was incapable of coldness in her dealings with even strangers, but though she was far from despising Yann, his deformity could, as he himself realised, do nothing to help her to find him attractive. Meanwhile, Yann hid his anguish in the intensity and skill of his playing, preserving a cheerful outward demeanour as he accompanied the dancing, a demeanour that masked the misery of his private thoughts.

Marie and Annette, seeking for a few moments of respite from the dancing and feasting, stole away from the happy throng and strolled in a secluded part of the garden. Marie, radiantly happy, turned to Annette and spoke to her sister.

"Annette, this is the happiest and most wonderful day of my life." She sighed contentedly. "To be married to the man I love, and to know that we shall be together for ever. What more could any woman want?"

Annette smiled. "I am so happy for you, dear Marie," she replied. "You know that I wish you and Paul all possible happiness. You have chosen well, I'm certain. He'll be a wonderful husband for you."

"And now, what about you, Annette?"

"What about me?"

"Come, don't play the innocent," laughed Marie. "You know perfectly well what I'm talking about. Where and who is your perfect husband? Where is your ideal lover, the man who will make you happy for ever and ever?"

"There is no one of such high merit at present."

"No one? Really, you are hard to please!"

"The man I shall marry will have to be…" and Annette paused a second. "Handsome. Of course! But that isn't all. He must be cheerful, patient, good tempered, kind, thoughtful, generous, tender, considerate, industrious…"

"Stop! Stop!" laughed Marie. "All the good things every girl looks for in a husband! And why not? But surely there must be someone you've met who possesses at least most of these desirable qualities?"

"Ah, but most of all…" replied Annette, giving an enigmatic smile. "Most of all, the man I shall marry will have some particular talent, in addition to all the other virtues. I want to be able to say proudly to people, when I'm married, 'You see that man? He is my husband.' And he will be outstanding for a talent that he possesses to a degree that makes him stand out. He will not be an ordinary man, but one who makes his mark, who stands out from the crowd."

"I hope with all my heart that you will find such a paragon," laughed Marie, "But I fear you aim too high."

"Time will tell. I'm in no hurry. I shall find such a man someday. Meanwhile this is not my happy day; it's yours. And your new husband will be wondering where his bride has disappeared to."

So they returned to the dancing.

It was after midnight when the last dance came to an end and the guests, collectively or in pairs, took their leave. Yann, tired by his exertions with the bow and by the conflicting emotions that the sight of Annette had rekindled in him, prepared to depart. Annette and her parents had sought Yann out and thanked him for his efforts. They offered him money, but he refused to accept any payment beyond knowing of the gratitude of his hosts, and with their renewed thanks echoing in his ears and a sad longing for Annette in his heart, he tucked his violin under his arm and turned his face to the homeward road. It was, fortunately, a moonlit night, for which Yann was grateful, since he had a long walk before him.

After a while, the path forked and he had to make a decision – should he turn right and continue along the main highway? This was a long way round, but he would have the moon to guide him. Or should he take the left hand turn, leave the highway and go through the woods? This was a much shorter route, but he would be much less guided by the moon. He thought for a moment then decided. He was tired, after all, and longed for his bed.

"I'll take the path through the wood," he finally told himself. "Then I'll be home in twenty minutes. If I go by the highway it'll take me nearer an hour."

He yawned from sheer fatigue, and this struck him as a good omen, suggesting that in choosing the route that would more quickly bring him home to his bed, he had chosen well. But suddenly an awful thought struck him. If he went through the wood he might, just might, meet the Korrigans. Now that was a terrifying thought. Nobody had ever set eyes on the Korrigans because they were creatures of the night, but everybody feared them. Yann sat down on a tree stump and considered. Again, he weighed up the advantages and the drawbacks of the two routes from which he had to choose, only this time he had to consider the possibility of an unwelcome encounter with those frightening little people. Again the effects of the exertions and the emotions to which he had been subjected during a long and busy day decided him. With another yawn, he opted for the short way. After all, he told himself, suppose the Korrigans didn't really exist? What if they were merely a figment of people's fevered imagination? With these thoughts, he gathered up his fiddle and tucked it under his arm, then heaved himself to his feet. Then he plunged into the dark and silent wood.

There was just enough light from the moon, filtering through the trees to enable Yann to keep to the path, and he had gone perhaps halfway through the wood when he imagined he could hear mysterious scuffling sounds, excited whisperings, and stifled laughter. Feeling less sure of himself now, and beginning to regret that he had not gone by the highway, Yann started to whistle a jaunty tune in order to keep up his spirits. Then the moon slid behind a cloud. Immediately the wood was bathed in a bright light, and Yann saw that he was surrounded by scores of little figures in strange costumes who jabbed their tiny fingers at him, dancing round him in excitement. As he stood rooted to the spot, he was suddenly grabbed by a number of them and led off through a dense hedge of trees and bushes. On emerging at the other side, Yann was aware of a large clearing before him, on the edge of which sat a Korrigan who was evidently of higher rank than the rest. Yann was led before this awesome personage, who looked him up and down as he spoke.

"Mortal man, who come unbidden into the land of the Korrigans, who are you? Where are you going? Why have you come to our wood?"

Yann explained politely, his heart thumping with terror, that he was a musician returning from a wedding and that, being tired, he had chosen the shortest and quickest route home.

The king of the Korrigans appeared not to be satisfied with this response.

"Why do you wish to harm us?" he enquired crossly.

"Harm you? Oh no, Your Majesty. That was never my intention. I wish only to be in my bed at home as soon as I may. I am only a humble musician and I -"

He was cut short by the king of the Korrigans.

"A musician, you said. Ah, yes. Very well. You shall play for us, for the Korrigans are as fond of dancing as are mortals. What say you, my friends?"

"A dance! A dance! The mortal man shall play for our dance!" They shrieked, jumping up and down in their excitement.

Yann's heart sank. He was well nigh exhausted, and longed for the blessed relief of sleep. Now he was being asked to play again. For how long? And then what would happen? Would he ever get away alive?

"Play for us, mortal man!" ordered the King.

Unable to do otherwise, Yann lifted his fiddle to his chin and drew his bow across the strings. To his amazement his fatigue left him instantly, like a cloak slipping from his shoulders; he felt strong and vigorous. No more did he long for his bed. He played and the Korrigans danced. Fast, slow, lively, gentle, prestissimo, largo, andante, allegro giocoso, maestoso... Yann played in every tempo, in every mood, in every key. He had never played with such consummate mastery before. The violin was bewitched! He played tunes he'd never heard before. He performed feats of violin playing that he didn't even know about, and all with no effort whatsoever on his part. His bow needed no guidance from him as it flew over the strings, his fingers ran up and down the fingerboard as if some enchantment were directing them. And all the time the Korrigans danced with unabated vigour and frenzy, laughing and screaming with delight, clamouring always for more. They seemed tireless, and their pleasure limitless. How long he played Yann could not tell, but eventually the King clapped his hands to bring the dancing to a halt, and signalled to Yann that his playing was to stop. Then he rose majestically and walked over to Yann.

"Mortal man," he intoned majestically. "You have entertained us most splendidly. Is that not so, my people?"

The Korrigans shouted, stamped their feet, and cheered, giving their wholehearted agreement.

"I think," went on the King, "That the mortal man, who has so delighted us must have a reward."

" A reward! A reward!" they screamed.

"Mortal man, you shall choose. We can give you whatever you desire. Do you choose wealth? Or rich clothing? Or costly jewels? Or maybe a sumptuous palace to live in? Servants, perhaps? Lands? What is to be your choice? Speak. Speak – tell us, mortal man."

Yann stood bewildered, completely at a loss for words, looking in a dazed way at the King and at the Korrigans who swarmed round him. Finally, gathering his wits, he spoke.

"I have no need of wealth, or palaces, or jewels. I am a simple man, and I have everything I need. I am happy if my playing has brought you pleasure. That is all."

"It cannot be all, mortal man," replied the King, looking keenly into Yann's face.

Then he walked slowly round Yann as he stood there, letting his gaze wander over Yann's shoulder and fix itself on his hump.

After staring fixedly at the hump for a short while, he again asked Yann, "Is there nothing, nothing at all, that you would like?"

He spoke slowly, his eyes still on Yann's deformed back.

A wild idea came to Yann, a foolish hope that the King might, just might, perhaps, be able to answer the prayer that had been in his mind, unspoken for as long as he could remember.

"I would like," he began, excited by an awareness of the

enormity of what he was asking. "I would like – that is, if it's not too much to ask – to be upright and straight, like a normal man, to be freed from this hump upon my back. Rather than gold or silver or fine possessions, if you could -"

In that instant the Korrigans vanished – the light that had illuminated Yann's capture, his questioning, the dancing, the promise of a reward, all were transformed into utter darkness – and Yann found himself again on the path that led out of the wood. To his astonishment, he realised that he no longer had a hump upon his back! He stood upright, tall and handsome, a hunchback no more. The tiredness he had felt earlier had returned, but he now went on his way with a light heart, and soon he was back home. He sank into his armchair, too tired even to undress and go to bed, and in a few seconds was fast asleep.

The sound of his gentle snoring aroused Gaspard from his fitful slumbers. He got up from his bed and went downstairs, groping his way in the darkness. From the doorway he awakened Yann with a surly shout, and demanded to know why he had returned so late.

"The Korrigans," mumbled Yann, drowsily. "I met the Korrigans… in the wood… I had to play for them… violin."

Then he slipped back into sleep. But Gaspard, now himself fully awake, demanded to hear more about his brother's adventure. Yann told him everything, concluding with the Korrigan King's offer of a reward. He told Gaspard that he had been offered wealth beyond imagining – and had refused it. Gaspard interrupted him angrily.

"They offered you money, and you turned it down?" he shouted. "Are you quite mad?"

But Yann was fast asleep once more.

In a blind rage, Gaspard suddenly seized Yann's violin and bow and stamped out of the cottage, scattering furniture and crockery in his clumsy progress. Guided by the moon, he made his way to the wood. He was determined to make good the serious mistake that his brother had made in refusing to accept money.

Just as Yann had done, Gaspard heard strange rustling

sounds and hushed voices. Like Yann, he was suddenly blinded by a light that scattered the darkness and revealed a host of strange figures who bore him off to the presence of the king in the clearing. Before long he found himself playing for the Korrigans to dance. He was no player, having not an ounce of the talent of Yann, but it did not matter, since the violin and the bow appeared to be bewitched, and Gaspard's playing pleased the Korrigans as much as Yann's had done. Gaspard too was eventually able to stop playing, and would doubtless have been offered the same rewards as Yann. But Gaspard cut short the King's recital of what he could give in return for the entertainment.

"My brother was here earlier," he said.

"That is quite true, mortal man," the King replied.

"I know what you offered him, and, fool that he is and always was, he rejected it."

"Go on, mortal man. Make your choice."

"I choose, then, to have what my brother did not want."

Immediately, the bright light gave way to utter darkness, the Korrigans vanished and Gaspard was alone. But the Korrigan King had been true to his word, and Yann's hump was now firmly set on Gaspard's back.

"Hooray!" shouted Jessie, as Pickle concluded his narrative. "It serves him right!"

"That's all very well," objected Velly. "At least, as far as it goes. What I want to know is -"

"Don't tell me," interrupted Pickle, with a knowing smile. "You are quite right to wonder, and it would be wrong to leave loose ends, wouldn't it?"

"What are you talking about?" queried Jessie, mystified at Velly's qualified praise for what she thought was a jolly good story with a highly appropriate ending. Poetic justice. That's what it was. Punishment for the wicked. The villain gets his just desserts. What more was there to be said?

Pickle continued to smile, and then he looked at Velly and said, "I'll tell you. The fact is that, as events turned out, Yann was left with a bit of a problem."

"Oh don't complicate matters, please," groaned Traffy. "The lad has just got shot of one problem. Don't give him another one."

Pickle turned deadly serious, and in solemn, theatrical tones said, "Yann's problem now was simply this – whom could he ask to play the music for the dancing when he and his Annette were married?"

"That tells me all I wished to know. Thank you," smiled Velly.

Georgie's Story

"There's the post, I do believe," cried Jessie, one morning at breakfast. "I'll go," she went on, as Velly moved to get up. "You finish your coffee, dear."

"Only one letter," she said, returning and resuming her seat. "It's from Michael and Harriet."

"Well, that's far, far better than a bill," commented Velly, who was always pleased to hear from their son. "What do they say, my love? Read it out."

Jessie put on her glasses and scanned the letter. "Oh, they've had a day in York, and they took the children to the museum and -"

"Which one?" laughed Velly. "York's full of museums."

"The big one, I suppose. Yes, the one with the Victorian street and the old things… and things," replied Jessie, vaguely. "Don't interrupt. Oh, they want to come and see us. Mike has a few days of holiday due, and they haven't seen us for a while, so -"

"When? And for how long?"

"Three weeks from now." She looked up from the letter. "Let's invite them to stay for a week. Our grandchildren are growing so quickly these days. It'll be lovely to see them again."

"Splendid idea. The boys tire me out, I admit, but it'll be a nice change. I'll give Mike a ring tonight."

"Lovely. So that's settled." She finished reading the letter and passed it over the marmalade jar to Velly. "By the way," she enquired, "Traffy and Pickle are coming round this morning, aren't they?"

"Yes. But not for another hour or so."

"Good. When we've finished the washing –up, I'll just have time to go round the music room with the duster and the vacuum cleaner before they arrive."

Velly sighed. As if Traffy and Pickle would notice a bit of dust...

"So what's the news of the day?" asked Pickle, as he checked the tuning of his violin.

"Nothing much," replied Velly. "There was a pheasant in the garden on Tuesday. And the hedgehog was back again last night. And Jessie says I need a new pair of slippers."

"That hardly counts as news," chortled Traffy, running off a frisky arpeggio. "By the way, I notice you've dusted the piano."

Velly studiously ignored this last remark, and merely replied, "Well, the only news – proper news – I have is that my son and his family are coming to stay with us next month."

"How many grandchildren have you?" asked Pickle, idly running his finger along the mantelpiece in a vain search for dust.

"Five altogether, but only two for this particular visit."

"I only have two grandchildren," said Pickle. "A little girl called Margie and a little lad called Georgie. He's an absolutely typical younger brother, full of mischief. But he's bright. You're looking very serious, Velly," he concluded, changing the subject rather abruptly.

"Yes," Velly returned. "It's that name, Georgie. It reminds me of a story I read a long time ago. In fact, I think it was when I was about ten or eleven. It was about a little lad called Georgie, and it was based, apparently, on a real-life case. It all happened about 1900 or 1920, I believe."

"Do I smell a story in the offing?" enquired Traffy.

"Yes, you do. I'm sure it will all come back to me. If I get lost or stuck I'll just improvise. I do remember the main outline clearly enough."

He paused, then resting his cello on the floor, he got up and went to the door. There he called out, "Jessie! Story time!"

"Coming!" they heard from the kitchen, and the next moment Jessie came bustling in, untying her pinafore before settling herself down in an armchair.

"Ready," she said. "Fire away!"

Frank Webb was not a wealthy man, but he had a steady job at the local factory that paid him reasonably well, and he was generally well liked as a gentle, sober, kindly, self-effacing sort of fellow. He and his wife Mary had one son, Georgie, and they lived, comfortably and contentedly enough, in an ordinary house in a 'good' part of Longfield St. John. Life was fairly settled for the little family, until suddenly, Reg found himself a widower with a six –year old son to bring up on his own. His beloved Mary had died in childbirth, along with the baby she was carrying. Reg was, of course, shattered by this loss, but with the help of kind neighbours and of his sister who lived near enough to be able to pop over most weekends, he had been able to keep going, though he found the effort of being both father and mother to young Georgie a strain. He soon came to the conclusion that he needed a wife as much as Georgie needed a mother. So he accepted the attentions of Edie Park, who lived a few doors away and was a widow in her mid-thirties. It is hard to say whether or not Reg had much genuine affection for Edie, or indeed to be sure whether it was she who courted him, rather than vice versa. People used to say that Reg was a rather weak man, a nice man, who needed a strong woman on whom he could lean in times of stress, even if she had to bully him from time to time. Mary had been just such a woman, but she had possessed in addition a warmth of character and a sense of humour, so that Reg was rarely put out whenever Mary, with affectionate firmness, gave him his instructions. Ideally Reg would have found another such person to marry, but he knew that a woman who would make the perfect wife for him would be virtually impossible to find. So he allowed himself to be won over by Edie, seeing in her the nearest he was likely to get to realising his ideal. She was a hard, sharp woman, whose firm, regular features made her attractive in a sort of way. But there was a coldness, a grimness about her, a lack of humour that would have deterred any man who was not actively seeking marriage. But Reg wanted a mother for Georgie, and Edie was available and more than willing. Hardened by adversity and not lacking in spirit, she saw in Reg a source of security, a settled future for both herself and her twenty-year-old son Roger. This young man was an unlovable ne'er-do-well, who had been in and out of work for several years. The prospect of becoming stepfather to Roger had been the one major factor that had given Reg pause for thought when he began frequenting Edie seriously, and he worried about the implications for Georgie of having Roger as a brother. However Edie, who was sharp enough to perceive these misgivings troubling the man she intended to marry, was able to sweet-talk him into resigning himself to any possible imperfections in the new family set up, and she played cleverly upon Reg's concern for Georgie's well-being, promising to be a good mother to him.

The first few months of his second marriage appeared to justify Reg's decision, but it gradually became clear that young Georgie was not happy. The reason was that Edie, having ensnared a husband to provide for her, was now beginning to show herself in her true colours. So indeed was her son. Roger had abandoned any ideas he might have had concerning the finding, and keeping, of a job of work. He preferred to stay at home during the day and to go out at night in the company of other like-minded young men, who were not too bothered about not keeping on the right side of the law if they could get away with it. He regularly arrived home in the early hours of the morning, most often the worse for drink, and would drag himself off to bed, where he would stay until his mother called him down to have some lunch. Edie no longer bothered to try to find out how Roger had spent his time. As for Reg, his tentative enquiries were met with curt and evasive answers, and the surly enjoinder that his stepfather could mind his own business.

"You're not my father," he would snap. "I don't have to listen to you. Leave me alone. I'll lead my own life without your help."

Edie's frustration at being unable to communicate with her son in a meaningful way began to manifest itself in increased hostility toward Georgie. She also felt resentful at the thought that by comparison with her own son, her husband's child was so amenable and biddable. It made her feel that she had failed as a parent, whereas Reg had succeeded. The consequent jealousy she felt did nothing to sweeten her temper. The more her son's imperfections were revealed to her, the more Georgie's constant goodness seemed to mock her, and she grew to hate the younger boy, whom she looked on as a sort of necessary baggage that came with his father. Many a time she would accuse Georgie and punish him for offences that had been committed by Roger. These included the theft of small sums of money, or of items that could be sold, even presents that Reg had given to Edie. It was easy for her to accuse her stepson, and she would make short work of dismissing Reg's ineffectual attempts to intercede on his son's behalf. On one occasion, Georgie was sitting reading under the table when Roger came in and, thinking that no one else was in the room, helped himself to some money that was in a tin on the windowsill. After replacing the tin, he turned round and happened to notice Georgie, who was pretending to have seen nothing, though he had actually witnessed the theft.

Roger dragged his young stepbrother out and, with his rough hands round Georgie's throat, almost choking him, spat out, "If you breathe a word I'll smash your stupid little face in, see?"

He then roughly released Georgie, and hurried out to join his mates. Edie soon discovered that the money was missing and immediately blamed Georgie, refusing to listen to his attempts to tell her the truth, and finally giving him a sound thrashing. Constantly persecuted in this way, Georgie became withdrawn and timid, spending more and more time sitting huddled in a corner of the sitting room when he came home from school, or going outside in order to escape from his stepmother.

He developed an interest in stamp collecting, and spent hours poring over an old album that Reg had found, meticulously organising his little collection and delightedly adding to it when Reg from time to time brought home stamps given to him by his colleagues at work, or purchased by Reg as a treat from the little stamp shop in town.

All this time, despite his miserable home life, Georgie had been working hard at school, and in due course his application to his studies won him a scholarship to the grammar school in the town. Reg watched proudly as the lad cycled off on the first morning, wearing his smart uniform. Edie was sneering and bitter about Georgie's success, and refused to share her husband's pride and happiness in it.

"Huh," she snorted. "He's just been lucky. You can't deny that. It's a pity we can't all have the chances he's had."

She would however have found it difficult to explain why she imagined that Georgie had had more chances to improve himself than Roger had had.

"Well, he has worked hard for it," said Reg, reflecting that he could name a certain young man who would do well to emulate his young brother's example.

"He'll come back full of big ideas about himself and about his station in life," she went on. "He won't have any time for us by the time he's finished his... education."

She spat the word out, and Reg meekly decided that there was no point in arguing with her over the rights and imagined wrongs of his son's achievement. So he said no more.

Despite Edie's hostility, Georgie enjoyed his first year at the grammar school. This was partly due to the fact that he struck up a friendship with Tom, a classmate who shared his interest in stamps. At home he was constantly harassed by Roger, who would maliciously seize Georgie's schoolbooks when he was doing his homework and hide them in the hope that Georgie would get into trouble as a result, as he did on more than one occasion. But Georgie always looked forward to going to school, since he enjoyed the lessons and his friendship with Tom.

"I'd love to see your collection," he said to Tom one day.

"I could bring my albums to school," replied Tom. "Well, maybe. It would be better if you could come to my house. Look, I'll ask my mum if you can come to tea one day. Shall I?"

"That would be super. I'd like that very much."

"I'll ask her tonight. I'm sure she'll agree."

Tom's mother did indeed agree, and so Georgie was invited to cycle over to Tom's house at Trimley, a village about eight miles away, the following Saturday.

Edie, though she did not actually object to Georgie's going out to tea, made it quite clear to him that she was doing him a big favour by granting her permission.

"You'd better behave yourself," she lectured him. "Don't go getting into any trouble or any silly scrapes. And," she added, shaking her finger in his face, "just make sure you're back here by nine o'clock. It'll be pitch dark at half past nine, and you've no lights on your bike yet."

"I'll see he has some lights on his bike next weekend," Reg said. "He'll be needing them anyway, as it'll be dark before he gets home from school in a few weeks."

"That doesn't help the situation for this Saturday, does it?" snapped Edie, turning on her husband. "I'm merely telling him to be back by nine on Saturday because at the moment he has no lights on his bike. Whether or not he will have lights on his bike in a week's time or a fortnight's time is neither here nor there. And I'll thank you not to interrupt when I'm telling your son what's for his own good."

"All right, my dear. All right. You're quite right," replied Reg meekly, anxious not to make an unpleasant situation worse.

"Now then, young man," she went on, turning to Georgie. "I hope you're listening to me. Back by nine o'clock, or you'll be in trouble. Do you hear me?"

"Yes, mother," Georgie replied, wishing that an event that promised such happiness did not have to be turned into an excuse for yet another ill-tempered lecture.

It was, in fact, nearly ten o'clock when Georgie returned home from his visit to Tom's. He had a black eye, his wrist was bandaged under his coat sleeve, and he was tired out.

But Edie was waiting for him. "And where do you think you've been, you ungrateful little wretch?" she stormed, accompanying this last word with a slap that sent Georgie reeling against the doorway. "What did I say to you about being back here by nine o'clock? Do you ever listen to anything I say to you? Do you think it's funny to be so deliberately and wickedly disobedient? And you've been in a scrap, I see."

"I can explain."

Georgie tried to get a word of explanation in, but Edie gave him another clout and ordered him off to bed. As he went out he turned appealingly to his father.

"Dad, I can explain. I'm late because -"

"All right, old son. Just get yourself off to bed. Best not to argue. You'll only make things worse."

And that was all Reg could say in the presence of Edie in the mood she was in. So Georgie took himself off to bed, dreading what would happen on the morrow, and wondering why he was always treated so unreasonably.

Reg and Edie were about to retire at about half past ten, when there was a knock on the door.

"I wonder who that can be at this time of night," said Reg.

"If you had the wit to go and open the door instead of just standing there wondering, you'd probably find out," was Edie's reply.

It was the police Sergeant. Reg ushered him in and, once inside, he came straight to the point.

"Are you the parents of Georgie Webb?"

"I'm his stepmother. He's the boy's father." And she indicated Reg.

"I hope you're proud of your son, Mr Webb. I'm sure -"

"If he's got himself into some kind of trouble," interposed Edie, "that's nothing to do with me, and I don't want to know. I told him quite distinctly to be back here by nine o'clock, and it was ten o'clock if you please, when he condescended to show his face. I told him it would be dark by half past nine – that's why I told him to be back by nine. He's got no lights on his bike, and now I suppose you've caught him riding without lights. That's it, isn't it?"

"Well, yes, Mrs Webb. I daresay he was, but -"

"Look, Officer." Reg tried to intercede on Georgie's

behalf. "I'm sure that if we could just -"

"And I'm sure," retorted Edie, "That you – not we – can sort out your son's problems. I'll say it again – if he's got himself into trouble with the police, then you can sort it out on your own. I'm going to bed." And she flounced out.

The sergeant watched her go in silence, took a deep breath, and was about to speak when Reg forestalled him.

"Look here, Officer. I'm sorry my boy was caught riding without lights, but surely there's no need to be too hard on him. I'll have a word with him in the morning, and it won't happen again. I've told him that I'll be buying some lights for him, anyway. Can't we just leave it at that?"

"Mr Webb, I would not expect you to be proud of your son if all he'd done was to ride his bike without lights after dark." He paused. "May I sit down?"

Reg nodded, fearing worse was to come, yet puzzled by the Sergeant's referring once again to his being proud of Georgie. The Officer seated himself and went on.

"It's like this, Mr. Webb."

And the truth came out, the real reason why Georgie had come home so late.

He had dutifully left Tom's house at about eight o'clock, giving himself plenty of time to cycle home in daylight. However, on arriving at the bridge at Coates Lane, some three miles from home, he had heard screams coming from behind the hedge that bordered the road. He got off his bike and cautiously went to investigate. An old lady had been dragged off the road and was being beaten by a ruffian, who demanded her money and valuables. Georgie realised, to his horror and dismay, that the assailant was his stepbrother Roger. Even so, he could not ignore the old lady's plight and so, small as he was, he threw himself on Roger and tried to drag him away.

"Your son acted very bravely, Mr Webb. He's only half the size of his brother, but he never hesitated when he saw what was happening to the old lady. Of course, he didn't stand a chance, and he'd have been in serious trouble if Roger had been allowed to see it through."

"So what happened?" Reg asked.

"Fortunately it happened that Dr Livesey was riding home from a visit to a patient out that way, and when Roger heard the sound of the horse's hooves approaching he made off, taking with him the money he'd stolen from the old lady, and pausing only to throw Georgie's bike into the river. The doctor stopped when he saw young Georgie and the state he was in, and the laddie told him what had occurred. He bandaged Georgie's wrist and bathed his eye for him. But he was unable to do anything for the old lady – she was already dead, as a result of both the beating she'd suffered, and shock."

"My God! So -"

"So, Mr Webb, we're talking about murder."

"But are you sure?" asked Reg, horrified at the thought of being involved, even if only at second hand, in a murder. "Are you quite certain it was Roger?"

"As certain as I need to be, I reckon," was the reply. "It was unfortunate that the doctor was not there a few moments sooner so as to be able to identify the attacker, but it was the doctor who found this at the scene of the crime."

He drew from his pocket a large and vicious-looking knife.

"Do you recognise this, Mr Webb?" he enquired.

"Yes. It's Roger's. I've never understood why he needs to own such a nasty weapon. But yes, that's his all right."

"Did it occur to you to wonder why young Georgie came home in such a state? The doctor, who incidentally, came straight to the police station, tells me the lad was badly hurt in the scrap. I'll need to talk to him some time soon. But it's late and I've one or two other enquiries to make, so I'll bid you goodnight. By the way, don't say anything to anyone about this until I've finished my enquiries."

The next morning, the Sergeant was back with two of his men. Edie, when shown the knife, had grudgingly and warily to admit it was Roger's. Roger had actually told her that he had lost it, and asked her to keep a look out for it. He even went so far as to accuse Georgie of stealing it. Now he had been roused from his bed and was being questioned by the Sergeant.

"Where were you last night, young man?"

"Here. At home. All evening."

"Is that true, Mrs. Webb?"

"Well..." Edie hesitated, uncertain how to answer for the best. "Yes, he was indoors for the whole of the evening, and I'm sure -"

"You see, one of your neighbours says that she saw your son leaving this house at about seven thirty."

He paused. Nobody spoke. The Sergeant turned to Roger.

"Another witness who'd been working on his allotment at Monks Cross until about seven forty five, testifies that you were passing the allotments just as he was about to leave. Now, there was an incident yesterday evening near the bridge at Coates Lane at about eight thirty. And..." he paused. "Your knife was found at the scene of the -"

"My son came home before nine o'clock!" Edie blurted out, anxious to protect her son. "He could not possibly have been at Coates Lane at eight thirty."

"Aha!" said the Sergeant. "So you admit that he was not, in fact, here all evening. That's your alibi demolished, my lad," he went on, looking hard at Roger. "Your memory, Mrs Webb, seems to be playing tricks with you. I think your son had better come with us to the station. There are a few more questions I'd like to put to him."

"But you can't just -"spluttered Edie, frantic.

"Mrs Webb, I am investigating a murder."

He paused to let the word sink in.

"So that's what you were talking about last night," said Edie, chastened. "I thought you were simply talking about cycling without lights."

"An elderly lady was attacked last night and robbed of money and some jewels, and she died as a result of the attack. Dr Livesey was unable to save her life. All the evidence, not to mention the testimony of reliable witnesses, points to this young man as our prime suspect. Take him away, you two," he said to his constables. "And keep him safe until I get back to the station."

Roger was led away, and the Sergeant continued.

"Oh yes. I agree that young Georgie, having retrieved his bike from the river, had to ride home without lights, but I'm certainly going to overlook that little misdemeanour in the circumstances. You, Mrs Webb, don't yet know why he was late returning, seeing that your husband has said nothing to you about our conversation of last night. But then you presumably didn't want to know anyway, did you?"

He then told Edie of the events he had outlined to Reg a few hours earlier. During his narrative, Reg came into the room.

As he concluded, the Sergeant turned to Reg and said, "I hope that from now on you'll take a bit more notice of young Georgie. He's a very brave lad, and a credit to you. And he's never breathed a word about what happened. The truth emerged only because the doctor spotted the knife at the scene of the crime."

"You're right, sergeant," Reg replied. "I ought to have listened to what he had to say last night when he came in, and to have asked him why he was in such a state. He must have been all in, poor old lad. I shut him up for the sake of peace."

Roger was found guilty of murder and sentenced to death. Edie, humiliated by the shame brought upon her by her son's disgrace, ashamed at the way she had treated Georgie, and unable to face her husband with her former assurance, hanged herself on the evening of her son's execution.

"What a jolly tale!" exclaimed Jessie, as Traffy launched into Chopin's Funeral March.

"What happened to Georgie in the end, I wonder?" said Pickle.

"And his father," replied Jessie. "Poor man. He really did need someone to look after him, didn't he?"

"He did indeed," said Velly. "Someone who'd make the odd cup of coffee for him and his mates at about eleven in the morning. That sort of thing, you know."

"Am I being got at?" queried Jessie.

"You, my sweet?" said Velly, giving her an affectionate squeeze.

"Right-ho. I'll bring some refreshments in now. But afterwards, when you finally get down to playing some music,

I shall sit in the comfort of that armchair and listen. I've done enough housework for today anyway."

"No hoovering to do?" asked Traffy, with a mischievous grin.

"No dusting?" asked Pickle.

I Hear You Calling Me

One day, as Pickle was tightening his bow, with his violin on his lap, he looked up and enquired of the others, for no particular reason, "How did you two first meet?"

"If you think there's a story there, you can think again," laughed Velly. "It was just a chance encounter. We weren't introduced or anything. We just happened to be both in the same place at the same time."

"But somewhere exotic and with music all round you, no doubt?"

"Not at all! First of all it was here – or, to be precise, up on the Height. And as for music – no, nothing."

"I expect the birds were singing," put in Traffy. "Though I don't recall for certain. But like Velly, I'd just gone out for a walk, and there he was. We had the place to ourselves, and we just got talking. One thing led to another and here we are."

"That's what happens when you talk to strange men," said Pickle, wagging his bow at Traffy. "My old mother, bless her, often used to warn my kid sister and me about it. Promise me you won't do it again, young man," he admonished, with mock severity.

"Oh, I don't know," countered Velly. "It would never surprise me to hear of a chance encounter with a complete stranger and a friendly chat, unearthing the details of a fine story. No, I'm all in favour of old codgers such as us three engaging in impromptu conversations."

"Now it's funny you should say that," remarked Traffy. "You're absolutely right, Velly. Three or four years ago as I recall, I chanced to meet an interesting old boy in the same way that I first met Velly. He was an ex-RAF chappie, and a most interesting fellow. He told me of a very odd experience he'd had some time previously. It was a sort of ghost story. Quite eerie, in fact. He'd been -"

"Stop!" exclaimed Velly, holding up his hand to halt Traffy's flow of words. He stood up, went to the door and called out to Jessie, "Story time!"

"What, already? You've not started playing yet!" came the reply from the kitchen. "Never mind. I'll come straight away, and you'll have to have the refreshments later, if that's all right."

"Just fine," Velly called back.

So Jessie came in, untying her pinafore on the way, and Traffy began his tale.

"I like the way you assume that I'm going to tell you this story," grinned Traffy. "I merely mentioned that I'd been chatting with this chap -"

"That's all we need," laughed Velly.

"Very well. I just hope I can remember all the details. It's probably best for me to put myself in the place of this ex-RAF type, and let him tell it in his own words. So, what I say to you is, as nearly as I can recall, what he actually said to me. This is his story."

My grandson and I have always been very close, and I've always enjoyed talking with him. We discuss all sorts of topics, and he asks me all sorts of questions, about people who were famous or in the news when I was a lad – sporting heroes mainly, but also statesmen and politicians who were household names to me but for him are merely names that come up in history lessons at school, or are mentioned in books that he reads. I'm quite happy to dig up the past in this way, especially as it brings back all sorts of memories for me and is interesting and informative to my grandson. He has a strong sense of history, has young Mark, and a love of the past that I find most unusual and very refreshing in a teenager. Anyway, one day, just after my seventieth birthday, he and I were chatting as usual about the old days, and we fell to thinking about the changes that had occurred in our everyday lives – very often as a result, direct or indirect, of the two great wars. I happened to mention the abolition of National Service in the late 1950s.

"National Service? What was that, Granddad?"

What a question! But it set me thinking about the war that I took part in, in the 1940s, as a young man. Sad memories came back to me, of hardship, suffering and personal loss. Happy memories too, of comradeship, courage, and heartwarming self-sacrifice. As I recounted these to young Mark, he listened, enthralled, never taking his eyes from my face.

As I paused for breath he said "You know, Granddad, you should write a book about all this."

"Oh, who'd be interested nowadays? It's only my memories, the memories of an old man. It's all in the past, and people want to forget awful things like wars, not to read about them."

"But it mustn't be lost for ever, Granddad," he replied, with an earnestness that impressed me. "I think it's important for people of my generation to know what your generation went through, and why you had to. It doesn't matter how long ago it was."

The lad was right, of course. The idea of writing a book about my wartime experiences suddenly appealed to me, I must admit. But what sort of book would it be? What would be the purpose of it? Who would be sufficiently interested to want to buy it, apart from people like Mark? The more I pondered over these and more practical questions, the less I felt inclined to pursue the idea of putting pen to paper. Yet at the same time, I felt a strange and growing urge, brought on by all this talk with Mark about my wartime life – to relive it, somehow. Then an idea came to me. I would go back to RAF Burnsworth, the bomber base where I had been stationed during the 1940s. I had, of course, no idea whether or not the base was still there – most likely not, in any form that I would recognise – but I could not shake off the nagging urge to get into my car and drive down there just to see. Odd, I thought, that it was, at least partially, practical considerations that deterred me from writing a book, yet here I was contemplating a journey that in practical terms was probably both foolish and pointless.

Anyway, a few days later I packed a small suitcase and announced that I was going away for a couple of days. My son and daughter-in–law, as soon as I told them the reason for my departure, came out with the reaction I had expected from my nearest and dearest.

"It's rather a long shot, isn't it?" was Sharon's comment. "Are you really serious about it?"

"Can't it wait a bit?" Colin asked. "I could maybe get a few days off next month, and I could come with you. Are you sure you're up to driving all the way there and back? Isn't it likely to be a complete waste of time in any case? There'll be nothing to see, Dad. The whole scheme is preposterous."

"Don't worry about me," I reassured them. "I'll be perfectly all right. I've got this bee in my bonnet, and I want to let it out. That's all."

"I wish I could come with you, Granddad. I hope you find the base and bring back some memories with you. If not, I hope you find the odd ghost. Enjoy your little excursion, anyway."

I'm bound to confess that it would have given me a lot of pleasure to have my grandson sitting beside me in the car. But ghosts? No. That's stretching the imagination a bit far, I thought.

So I drove off. I'd had a good look at the map the previous evening, and I knew pretty well where to find the base if it were still there.

The drive was a long one, and rather tiring, but I eventually arrived at Burnsworth. I recognised at once the High Street on its gentle slope, with the little café – now under a new name but still a café – where we used to pop in now and then for a cup of tea and a bun. There was the old Town Hall, and the Parish Church. Woolworths was still there in its old place, but the dear old Bijou cinema had gone. Of course, virtually all the shops were new and different. The base had been, I knew, just outside the town on some heathland on the east side, over the river and just past a little wood.

Naturally the wood had long since gone, buried under a large housing estate of the sixties, virtually a new town in itself. I parked the car and looked round. The estate sprawled over the entire area that the base had occupied and more, so that not a trace of it remained. There was not a Nissen hut in sight, not a yard of runway, not a scrap of rusty fencing, and I looked in vain for a windsock fluttering at its pole. It was getting late now, and the dusk was coming on. I felt, I admit, a little stupid. My son and his wife had been right. Why had I not at least made some enquiries, by telephone maybe, about the existence or otherwise of the base? I said to myself that I was a silly old man; how stupid to come all this way, on a fool's errand, on the strength of what was merely a passing whim! But I had wanted to come here, and I had done so, and in that sense at least I felt a certain satisfaction. I got out of the car and had a stroll round. I soon found a small hotel quite near where I was parked, so I decided to spend the night there and set off for home, chastened and somewhat ashamed, the next morning.

"Oh yes, this is where the RAF base used to be. As a matter of fact, I understand that this hotel is actually standing on the site of the canteen," laughed the landlord.

Well, it was, I suppose, appropriate enough, since I had just enjoyed an excellent evening meal.

The landlord went on. "Of course, by the time I first came here it had all long since disappeared, but some of the older locals used still to talk about the airmen they'd seen around in the old days." He paused. "And," he went on, "there are some streets on the estate that are named after wartime heroes, including one who was actually stationed here. I couldn't tell you his name, though. But that's about all. If you didn't know there'd been an RAF station here during the war, you'd not be aware of it from what you can see now."

Yes, indeed, it was difficult, when one looked at the rows of identical houses, to visualise the comings and goings of Lancaster bombers, the erks scurrying round keeping the planes airworthy at all times – the petrol tankers, the windsock on its pole, the continual to-and-fro of personnel in uniform or overalls, WAAFs and airmen. But I had been there – I had been part of it. I remembered.

I bade the landlord goodnight and went up to my room. I lay back in an armchair, closed my eyes, and allowed the memories to come back to me.

I must have dozed off, and I came to with a strange feeling that I was not alone in the room. Music was playing, softly, a soothing tune of the thirties. I opened my eyes and saw a smart young uniformed airman standing at the far end of the room. A bright moon cast its pale light on him. The words of an old song, familiar from long ago, came clearly to me:

> *"I hear you calling me.*
> *You called me when the moon had veiled her light,*
> *Before I went from you into the night.*
> *I came (do you remember?) back to you*
> *For one last kiss beneath the kind stars' light."*

And then I was aware that there was another person in the room, an attractive young woman, a WAAF. I just sat there, too amazed to speak or to move, and waited for whatever might happen next.

The girl spoke.

"Jack," she whispered. "Oh, Jack. I had to come and see you, before you -"

"Before I went from you into the night," came the words of the song. Then the airman spoke.

"And I was desperate to see you, my dearest, if only for a few brief seconds."

He held her close to him, tenderly. Then the scene darkened, as though the moon had slipped behind heavy clouds. The airman looked up at the sky.

"It's a big show tonight, that's all I know," he said. "We take off shortly to go and give Hitler a pasting he won't forget. I just hope this cloud cover stays so there'll be no moonlight to help them see us. Either way, this particular sortie is going to be unpleasantly dangerous. Goodbye, my darling. Be good while I'm away."

And he gave her a gentle peck on the cheek.

Again, the song:
"I came (do you remember?) back to you
For one last kiss...."

Then I remembered who these two were. The airman was Jack
Miller, with whom I'd played countless games of chess to pass
the time between missions. Jack the talented pianist who'd
entertained the whole station with his easy expertise at the
keyboard of the jangling old station piano. Jack the handsome
keep-fit fanatic, the Cambridge cricket Blue, the footballer, the
swimmer. No wonder all the WAAFs adored him. Jack was the
pilot of one of the Lancasters in our flight. I had been his
navigator on several missions before being transferred to a
different crew. And the girl? I had good reason to remember
her. But that comes later.

Then the ghostly lovers parted, and the whole scene faded.
I was left staring at the wall of my hotel room.

I must have nodded off again, slumped in my comfortable
armchair. But once again I awoke with the curious sensation
that someone else was also in the room. Opening my eyes, I
saw once again the same airman, standing exactly where he
had been before. This time however, he was wearing his flying
leathers. His face was streaked with blood, and most of the left
sleeve of his jacket had been torn off, exposing a deep, ugly
and bloody wound on his arm. He spoke gently but urgently.

"Stay there, Alice. Don't move."

And he raised a warning right hand. I realised then that the
girl was there too again, that she was sobbing convulsively and
at the same time laughing.

"Jack," she sobbed. "Oh, Jack! You've come back! We
were told you'd all been blown up over Germany. They said
the whole crew had died. But you're alive... It is really you,
isn't it, Jack?"

Again the words of the song:
"I came (do you remember?) back to you..."

"Don't touch me, Alice."

"But why not, Jack? Let me hold you..."

And she suddenly darted forward to throw her arms round him. But the instant her outstretched arms touched him, he vanished, and she was left clutching at empty air. Then, even as I watched, she too vanished.

I recalled then that fateful mission all those years ago. I remembered how the treacherous moon had suddenly burst through the clouds as we took off. I was one of the lucky ones. The pilot of the Lancaster I was flying in as navigator managed, somehow, to get us back to England. Jack's Lancaster had been blasted out of the sky, and the entire crew blown to pieces.

After the war, Alice and I became friendly, and eventually we were married. I never, ever, asked her how much she missed Jack, or to what extent I was, for her, only a second-best. She was always a loving and devoted wife and mother to me and to Colin.

Before leaving Burnsworth I located the street on the housing estate that had been named after Jack, and I drove slowly down it for old time's sake. Then as I drove home, I thought about how much I would tell my family of all that I had seen and heard in that hotel room. Would they believe me? Would they think I was beginning to do go soft in the head in my old age? More than likely! I hoped though that young Mark believed in ghosts.

Somehow, I felt sure he would.

I know I do.

Traffy stopped. "Thirsty work, this storytelling, isn't it?"

Jessie jumped up. "Well," she said. "You usually play some music before you start on the stories. Mind you, I think Traffy has done us proud, and I hope that after all the ghostly business you're now in the mood for music."

"No problem," Velly assured her, "Once we've got some coffee inside us, and -"

"All right, all right," Jessie said, laughing. "I know when it's time for me to go and make myself useful. But while I'm making the coffee you'd better decide what you're going to play. Something appropriate." And off she went.

"Powerful stuff, that story of yours," commented Pickle, who had been obviously moved by Traffy's tale. "And it's amazing, isn't it, what you hear when you start talking to strange men? Perhaps my old mum was wrong after all."

"Circumstances alter cases, they say," declared Velly. "But there's no doubt that on this occasion, Traffy happened to come across someone with an interesting – nay fantastical – story to tell. And 'good for him', I say."

When Jessie returned with coffee and biscuits she set the tray down on the little table and asked;

"Didn't Beethoven write a Ghost trio?"

"So he did," answered Pickle. "But that was long before the war. Still, that shouldn't stop us playing it. After coffee."

The Fate of Market Withercross

"I'm sorry. I always get that bit wrong," lamented Velly. "I think it's because of the change of key."

"There's an awkward cross-rhythm just there as well," added Traffy. "My part's a bit tricky too."

"Shall we go back to bar 57?" suggested Pickle. "That's where I come in after three bars rest. That bit that bothers you, Velly. Now," he went on. "Listen out for this descending figure in the violin part. This bit." He played the bar in question. "Then we come in together after two bars, while Traffy is busy twiddling away on the piano."

"Bar 57 then," Traffy confirmed. "3, 4, then you're in."

"Hang on a second," pleaded Velly. "Let me just have a look at that trouble spot. Hmm," he added, after a pause. "I think I know where I'm going wrong. It's one of those places I'll really have to practise."

"Mark it with a cross," advised Traffy with a grin.

Pickle, who had been on the point of saying something useful, instead broke off and uttered a loud guffaw.

"I say," he chortled. "You'll never believe this."

"Believe what?" demanded Velly, who was frowning over the cello part of the Brahms.

"When Traffy said 'mark it with a cross', I was reminded of a lovely little country village I used to know many years ago. It was actually called Market Withercross, believe it or not."

"I don't suppose there's a story connected with this rural idyll?" enquired Velly.

"There most certainly is. Shall we just finish what we're doing on this movement first? It'll be time for a break then, anyway."

"Excellent idea," said Velly. "I'm not going to let this little problem here defeat me, so we'll bash on. But I look forward to hearing about Market Withercross."

He laid his cello carefully on the floor and went over to the door.

"Jessie!" he called. "Story time in five minutes!"

"Coming!" she called back from the kitchen. "With coffee, of course. And," she added, "I've got some scones too, just out of the oven."

The three men looked at one another, and grinned, returning to the Brahms trio with renewed vigour.

Pickle put down his cup and cleared his throat. "Ah yes," he began. "Market Withercross. It was a quiet, peaceful little spot, miles from anywhere. Just a collection of stone cottages, a couple of shops, an ancient church surrounded by rolling farmland where corn grew and cattle grazed. A busy little stream ran through the middle of the village, under a picturesque old stone bridge. Rarely did anything happen to disturb the idyllic peace that reigned there – indeed, the ringing of the church bells on a Sunday and the quacking of the ducks on the pond, these were the characteristic sounds of the village. That, you see," explained Pickle, "was the sort of place we're talking about. That's how Market Withercross was, and everyone was happy."

Well, nearly everyone.

One day, a retired Army man, Major Waveney-Clinton, one of the oldest inhabitants, received a visit from his old friend Dr Withersley, who was in a state of agitation that was unusual for him.

"Have you heard the rumour, Rupert?" he asked the Major.

"What rumour? I've heard nothing. What's it about?"

"This proposed development."

"What development? Where?"

"Well, here! Here in Market Withercross."

"I say, Algy. This isn't on. Bad show, what? Look here, sit down, and I'll fetch some brandy. Now, what's all this nonsense? Who's behind it? We can't have any development here! Dash it all, it wouldn't be right."

"That bounder Lord is behind it."

"Might have guessed. What an infernal pest that man is."

"Damned upstart. Always on the make. I suppose it's to be expected of him."

"Yes, I daresay," barked the Major. "But we can't just let it happen. Give me the details, will you, and we'll work out some plan of campaign to stop the blighter."

This Mr Lord was a local farmer who owned a lot of land around the village, land that had been in his family for several generations. Frank Lord had inherited it, and all the wealth it brought, on the death of his father six years earlier. Now he had decided to realise the money that his fields and woodlands would bring him by selling off certain portions of them to speculative builders who intended to build a housing estate and some shops to serve it. The land that Mr. Lord was proposing to sell included the allotments that had been cultivated for over a hundred years, the cricket field, and some farmland that adjoined the little estate of Market Withercross Manor, the home of Major Waveney-Clinton and his family. The old soldier was displeased by both the idea of losing the superb views over green fields that his home enjoyed, and also the thought that the peace and quiet isolation of the village would be lost forever if so much of the land surrounding it were built on.

Mrs Waveney-Clinton, who came in at that moment, having heard raised voices in the drawing room, was rather less disturbed by the news than her husband had been.

"It simply means a bit of modernising," she said placidly. "Bringing the village up to date. Be reasonable, dear. People have to live somewhere, so houses have to be built. And then you need shops to cater for them. And other things, I suppose."

"That may well be true," snapped the Major. "But these things don't have to happen here, do they, for God's sake?"

Doctor Withersley, seeing a family row brewing and not wishing to be involved, attempted to pour oil on troubled waters, though he was hampered in this by the fact that he sided very strongly with the Major.

"There's something in what you say, Madeleine, and of course I'm not opposed to the building of houses for people to live in, in general terms. But not here. It would be totally inappropriate, so foreign to the whole spirit of the place. It would change the village forever. You can never bring back the real character of a place once its fields and woods have been built on."

"But what is the real character of Market Withercross?" asked Mrs Waveney-Clinton. "Surely it's changing all the time. It evolves as the years pass and people come and go. We shan't be here forever. Future generations may want to see more shops and houses and other amenities that we just don't have now."

"Then let them deal with it as and when they wish!" retorted the Major. "It'll be their problem, their choice, their concern. But it certainly is not ours. Don't you see that if Lord has his way we'll lose the cricket field? The allotments? They're both on his land, you know."

"Couldn't other sites be found for them?"

"Maybe. Maybe not. But why the hell should it have to come to that?"

The Major, having let off steam and paced about the room for a while, finally calmed down somewhat, muttering truculently.

"I shall fight this," he concluded. "Lord has not heard the last of this."

"It's sure to be no more than an idea at this stage, anyway," his wife pointed out. "He wouldn't just give the go-ahead to the builders behind everybody's back. He couldn't. Don't expect the bulldozers to be sent in just yet. In any case, he'll need to have planning permission. He can't just go ahead regardless."

But the Major refused to be placated. "I don't trust the blighter, Madeleine," he growled. "Don't trust him an inch. Nor do I trust those folks at the Town Hall. They don't live here, and they're as likely to be sympathetic to him as they are to see our point of view. Huh."

Later that day, in Market Withercross's general store, where, as in all good village stores, practically every item of everyday necessities could be found, Joanne Waveney-Clinton was engaged in conversation with Tommy, the young man who owned and ran the establishment, and Sally Simpson, who managed the Post Office side of the business. The major's daughter had called in to buy some stamps and a couple of birthday cards, and she had taken the opportunity to sound out Tommy and find out what were his views on the proposed development.

Tommy was cautiously optimistic about it, seeing the potential offered by an influx of extra population for increased trade and the possibility of expansion into bigger premises. He was, after all, a man with a business to be promoted. Joanne, however was, in this respect at least, her father's daughter, and she pointed out to Tommy that any new building on the scale proposed would completely destroy the character of the village. She reminded him, knowing him to be one of the stalwarts of the cricket club, that the field on which they played all their home matches would disappear under bricks and mortar and several tons of concrete. Tommy had not been aware of that fact, and it gave him pause for thought. However, he still fancied the idea of attracting more custom to his shop. To this Joanne replied that the very opposite might well prove to be the case.

"More houses doubtless bring more potential customers," she said. "But how can you be sure that they'll be your customers? There'll be new shops opening up to cater for the new population, and if those shops are conveniently sited, people will go there to make their purchases rather than here. So you could easily find yourself losing custom, not gaining it."

Again, Tommy had to admit that he hadn't thought of that. Sally who, seated behind the Post Office counter, had been listening to the conversation, was worried. When Joanne had departed, she came and added her views to the debate. She warned Tommy to be very wary, and to be sure to examine thoroughly all sides of the argument over the proposed new buildings.

"There are points for and against," she said. "We need to take into account all the pros and cons. Don't think there'll only be the question of how much new business it may bring you. It may, as Joanne was saying just now, turn out the other way. And don't forget that -"

She stopped suddenly, and a half-smile spread over her face.

"Forget what?" queried Tommy.

"It's just clicked with me," replied Sally. "Now, that could be very interesting. Very interesting indeed."

"What could?" asked Tommy, mystified. "What are you talking about?"

"It's Joanne. You know she's going out with Richard, don't you?"

"Richard? Oh yes – Richard Lord. Mr Lord's son! Of course! Now, I wonder how serious that little romance is. And what difference this new situation will make."

"I'll say this," returned Sally. "If Mr Lord's eldest boy, Charles, were Joanne's young man, they'd definitely be splitting up! That lad is his father all over again, just as Joanne is very like her father. Those two wouldn't be able to stay together as friends! But Richard's very different. I quite like Richard. He takes after his mother more. He's not a money-grubber, like Charles.

"Time will tell," answered Tommy.

"I've a suspicion that Joanne won't allow Richard too much of that," replied Sally. "I'm sure she'll get to work on him, in no uncertain terms. They're very fond of each other, I do know, but I can't see Joanne having anything to do with the son of a man who wants to do what Mr Lord has in mind – unless he's prepared to go against his father, that is," she added.

Joanne's brother John was discussing the prospects for the coming cricket season with Richard Lord. The two had long been good friends, though both were conscious of a new uneasiness in their relationship. Each tried to hide this unwelcome restraint behind their shared enthusiasm for cricket. The subject of the possible loss of the home ground was studiously avoided, and with the first match of the new season a mere fortnight away there were plenty of other matters to discuss – the new vice-captain, the parlous state of the pavilion, the retirement of the regular wicket-keeper, his likely replacement, the balance of the bowling in the side. Both were impatient for the season to begin, and both were privately hoping that the cloud hanging over the club would just quietly float away and leave well alone.

Joanne joined them on her way back from the Post Office. She greeted Richard with unwonted coolness, since her mind was still preoccupied with the problem of how to reconcile what Mr Lord was planning with the fact that his son was her boyfriend. John, uncertain whether he was being tactful or tactless, excused himself and walked away.

"Richard?" Joanne asked firmly, after an awkward pause. "How serious is your father about this?"

"You mean… about selling off his land?"

"What else?"

Joanne was as angry as Richard was embarrassed. But she wanted to know the truth of the situation, and Richard if anyone should be able to give her all the details. More importantly, since they were all but engaged, she needed to know Richard's feelings.

This rather put Richard on the spot. He was not of a naturally rebellious nature and had never in the past felt the need to go against his father's wishes. He was, as Sally Simpson had correctly assessed him, a decent lad, and he had none of his father's love of money – unlike his elder brother. He was sensitive, cheerful, a touch on the shy side, and he loved the countryside and outdoor pursuits. At twenty years of age, halfway through his university course, he was also very much in love with Joanne. To be truthful, she was equally fond of him. But as she in her practical way pointed out to him, their relationship would be under an intolerable strain if Mr Lord were to go ahead and destroy an environment that was so dear to her. She therefore, in effect, gave Richard an ultimatum – he must choose between her and his father. No compromise was possible.

But what could Richard do, poor lad? He could not realistically entertain any reasonable hope of being able to persuade his father to call off his projected deal. Neither could he give up Joanne without a fight. He was, of course, wholly on Joanne's side. He wanted exactly what she wanted, but what good would it do to defy his father, or to attempt to persuade him not to go ahead? Richard was quite clear that any such attempt was a non-starter.

This conversation between the two lovers caused both of them much distress. Richard moped in impotent anger, and Joanne went home and cried in her bedroom.

Not everyone in the village shared the Major's view. Tommy the shopkeeper had given a lot of thought to the likely effect on his business of an influx of newcomers and to the 'modernising' effect of a mass of new housing. He had come to the conclusion that, on the whole, the benefits to him at least outweighed the disadvantages. Slightly. Behind her grille, Sally would hear various comments from anxious and bewildered villagers throughout her working day. There was talk of legal action. A public meeting in the village hall had been called by the Major. Mr Lord had been invited to attend, to put forward his case and to clarify certain points, but had declined the invitation, preferring to leave such matters to his legal team.

Then came a report that made everyone sit up and take notice. Mr Lord's wife had threatened to leave him.

It was Easter Day. Mrs Lord had gone away for a few days to stay with her sister and to think things over. She had never believed that her husband would ever sell off his land for building, and his decision to do just that now struck her as a sort of betrayal. It was from her that their son Richard had inherited his love of the great outdoors, and to Mrs Lord, the fact that she lived in a spacious house with a big garden, surrounded by open country, was one of the greatest joys imaginable. Now her husband was intent, it seemed, on destroying that. And he had been adamant. Every time she had tried to discuss his plans with him, he had refused to discuss the matter. It was, he said, quite simply a business deal: end of conversation. So angry, hurt and frustrated, she had packed a small suitcase and driven over to her sister's for a stay of indefinite duration.

On the evening of his wife's departure, Frank Lord was sitting in unhappy solitude, mulling over what had been said on both sides in the course of the argument he had had with his wife. It had been a very heated argument, and it was obvious that the two opposing points of view would brook no compromise or reconciliation. Suppose she decided never to come back? But damn it, he was a businessman – surely he could buy or sell a few acres of land without having to secure everyone's permission first? But he did not fancy living without his Elizabeth. Their eldest son Charles would back him up, he knew. He was less sure of Richard, but the boy had never yet defied him. Pity about his fondness for that Waveney-Clinton girl, but there it was. Business could be cruel, and if one always considered the human cost then nobody would ever make a profit in any business deal. All the same, the house was already beginning to feel less friendly with Elizabeth not there. How long would she be away? He retired to bed a troubled, unhappy man.

That night, Mr Frank Lord had a dream.

In this dream he was sitting in luxurious ease in the back of his chauffeur-driven gold-plated Rolls Royce, being driven slowly and majestically down the wide main street of a new town. It was *his* town; it was he who had planned it and built it, putting up imposing buildings and rows and rows of houses where once had been green fields and woodlands. As he passed along the street, women and girls stopped to curtsey to him, while men and boys turned to bow or doff their hats. All the other traffic stopped to allow his car to pass. The sun shone, the trees and manicured lawns in the park and along the streets provided a pleasant green backdrop, and a big ornamental fountain splashed noisily in the centre of the main square. He, Frank Lord, had achieved all this – he, Frank Lord, was responsible, through his vision and business acumen, for creating this earthly paradise. He leaned back in the leather-covered luxury of his car, casually waving to acknowledge the greetings of the people. He closed his eyes and thought what a wonderful fellow he was. Soon, lulled by the gentle motion and quiet soothing hum of the car, he fell into a deep sleep.

When he awoke he was no longer in his car; he was walking. The sun was no longer shining, the sky was covered by dark lowering clouds and it was raining. Looking round where he was walking, he saw empty shops whose windows had been smashed and boarded up. There was litter lying all around him. A drunk came staggering out of a doorway and nearly knocked him over, passing on with a curse. Obscene graffiti covered the walls. A burnt-out car stood in the road. A police siren wailed. An old man, talking half to himself and half to anyone else who cared to listen, was gibbering a stream of inconsequential chatter, in the middle of which Lord was hit by the sentence, "I remember this place when it was all green fields". That was the only sensible thing the old man seemed able to say. Lord walked on past neglected, decaying houses. A tart standing at a street corner called out to him as he walked blindly past, "Want a good time, love?" but he ignored her. A gang of youths was coming towards him. He stepped off the pavement to let them pass, but they stopped, and as two of them grabbed his arms, the others began to beat him. He was thrown to the ground. Kicks and blows rained down on him and he was powerless to resist. He felt himself slipping into unconsciousness...

He awoke with a start from the nightmare and sat up in bed, thrashing about with his arms and legs and crying for mercy. Gradually, his mind cleared. He realised that he was in his own home in Market Withercross. But then where was Elizabeth? Ah, yes. Now he remembered.

Frank Lord knew that sleep would not return to his pillow that night, and that he would probably not welcome it if it did, so he got up and went downstairs. Over a cup of strong tea, he pondered over the dream and what it might mean.

He thought of the wealth that the sale of his land would bring him. But what was the point of it if Elizabeth was no longer there to share it with him? He thought of the break-up of his marriage. He thought of the misery his own son Richard would suffer if Joanne were to leave him, as she surely would. He thought of the cricketers' dismay at the loss of their ground, the anger of the allotment-holders who were now threatening legal action. He also saw now, for the first time, the damage he would do to the village, to the community. Even his own house would be affected if the beautiful views it commanded were lost. And suddenly these things mattered to him as never before. The memory of the first part of his dream now struck him as hollow, vainglorious and selfish, the second part likely to be a horrifying glance into a crystal ball. No, he'd been thinking only of himself. He could not let this development go ahead; it was a ghastly mistake for all sorts of reasons. He resolved to phone his solicitor as soon as the working day began. He also resolved to phone his sister-in-law and speak to his wife as a matter of urgency.

Frank Lord was, like Scrooge, a changed man. His name soon became a byword in the village for philanthropy. He paid for the building of a new cricket pavilion, had a new fence erected at the gardeners' request round the allotment site, arranged for necessary repairs to the roof of the village hall to be carried out at his expense. But he was very careful in all his good works to ensure that nothing would change the essential character of the village. In this he was always assisted by his wife, with whom he had been quickly reconciled. Joanne and Richard announced their engagement, and even the Major's wife agreed that everything had turned out for the best.

"And they all lived happily ever after," sang Jessie.

"I'm sure they did," agreed Pickle. "And why not?"

There was a brief silence then Velly asked, "What are we going to play now? Some more Brahms?"

"I'm in the mood for something rural," said Traffy. "All this talk about the goings-on in a little country village makes me feel quite... quite... What's the word?"

"Rustic?" suggested Pickle. "Bucolic? Pastoral?"

"Well, yes. Something like that. I know – what about that piece by Haydn that's got the Gypsy Rondo in it? You know the one I mean?"

"Certainly. I suppose that thinking about the countryside reminds you of gypsies, Traffy? Well, why not?"

"But I really must practise that bit of the Brahms that we were playing earlier," confessed Velly. "I don't want to be caught out next time we go through it. I hope, though," he added, with a rueful smile," that I can remember exactly where the trouble spot was."

"Well," said Pickle helpfully, "when you do find it you'll have to..." And he paused, with a mischievous grin – "... mark it with a cross."

"And we'll all live happily ever after," added Jessie, collecting up the mugs and plates.

Velly raised his eyes to Heaven. "Let's make a start on the Haydn, shall we?"

A Complicated Family Business

"I was reading somewhere the other day," said Velly, as the trio paused between the movements of a Haydn trio, "that in J.S. Bach's lifetime there were allegedly from twenty-five to thirty Bachs holding posts as organists, and they were all related to one another."

"That's quite a family of organists," commented Traffy.

"I find that a remarkable statistic," put in Pickle. "I mean, you can understand two, or possibly three, brothers, or cousins –"

"Or fathers and sons."

"Well, yes. Why not? But surely, to have over twenty is really rather remarkable."

"How many organists would there be in any town, though?" asked Velly. "In Germany, I mean, and in the eighteenth century."

"Goodness knows," replied Pickle. "But in any case, it's still a remarkable record for one family."

"Families are often surprising, though, aren't they?" asked Traffy. "I mean, for all sorts of reasons."

At this point Jessie came bustling in.

"Have you boys finished for the moment?" she enquired.

"If you mean 'is it coffee break time?' the answer has to be 'not just yet'. We've got one more movement of this Haydn to do, then I'm sure we'll all be ready for a cup of your most delicious, my dear."

"Right. I'll leave you for a few minutes."

"You know, I've a strange feeling, I confess, that there's a story somewhere in all this talk of families," said Velly. "In fact, one is coming back to me now in dribs and drabs. It's very complicated. Look, I'll tell you what we'll do – let's play this last movement of the Haydn, and then Jessie can join us for coffee."

"And storytelling," added Jessie, pausing on her way to the kitchen.

"Of course," promised Velly. "I reckon I'll have got my tale together by then. Medieval it is. Definitely medieval."

"Of the Middle Ages," declared Pickle. "Well, I reckon we're all middle aged, so it should suit us. Meanwhile, let's do our worst to Papa Haydn."

Ten minutes later they were all sipping coffee, and Velly began his story.

Sir Roger had still not fully recovered from the shock of the death of his beloved wife, though more than ten years had passed since she had been taken from him. How different a man he was now from the young tearaway who had once earned for himself the nickname of Roger the Reckless! But why, in his youth, should he care what people thought or said of him? He was only the second son; his elder brother Richard would inherit not only the family home and lands, but also the responsibilities that went with them. So Roger had lived life to the full, enjoying the thrill of hunting from which he would return, tired but exhilarated, to round off the day roistering in the tavern with his boisterous friends and the pretty, scheming wenches whom he was sure to find there waiting for him. Richard, his brother, was by complete contrast, a serious and quiet man, very conscious of his future role as Lord of the Manor, master of the estates and the people who helped to run them. He was, people would say, a reincarnation of his father after whom he was named – for Sir Richard was also a quiet man, fair in all his dealings with others, and disinterested in dispensing justice whenever his workers appealed to him to settle their disputes. He was not a strong, authoritative man, but humble and kindly in his ways, for which he was loved and respected by all, especially since a fever had carried off his wife while she was still a young woman. The servants and farm workers were all agreed in blessing their good fortune in not only having so good a lord and master, but also in being able to look forward with confidence to the same sort of agreeable governance that they could expect when Sir Richard should be taken from them and young Richard would inherit. Accordingly they were indulgent toward Roger, excusing his wild ways and irresponsible light heartedness. It did them no harm, and anyway, why should the lad not enjoy himself since his brother obviously had, as they used to put it, enough sense for both of them? Even old Sir Richard seemed to share their view. He and young Richard were inseparable, and the old fellow was as eager that his heir should know all that was necessary for the smooth running of his future inheritance, as Richard was to learn. This left Roger free to live his life as he pleased. Had his mother lived, it may be that he would have been different, but his nurse had no more authority over him than had his father.

Then, in a spirit of seeking adventure, Roger had on a sudden impulse decided to join the hosts who were marching off to unknown dangers and the chance of glory in the Crusades. His father and his brother showed mild surprise when he announced his intentions to them, but they made no effort to prevent his going. They were more than likely secretly relieved to see the departure of 'Roger the Reckless', whose reputation hardly brought glory to the family; maybe he could make himself a credit to them by deeds of valour in the fight against those insolent Saracens. Roger was just thirty years of age, a man without a care in the world, and having no ambitions other than to live life to the full and to seek adventure wherever he might find himself.

This was all in the past, the long-gone past. Sir Roger, as he now was, sighed as he thought back to those distant days, reflecting on the great change that had come about in him as a result of his experiences in the Holy Land. The carnage he had witnessed, the hardship he had had to endure over a decade, had made him take stock of his life, his plans – or lack of them – his future, his attitude toward the sufferings and difficulties of others. He saw the emptiness of his own hedonistic existence in which he cared for nobody but himself. On his return from the Crusades, he had surprised everyone by his changed demeanour, and his new maturity was a constant topic of comment among his father's household staff and workers. It was particularly pleasing to both his father and his brother, so that a new closeness developed between the three of them. Old Sir Richard knew that he was dying, and in due course he passed quietly away, peacefully and without regrets, three months after Roger's return. Richard duly came into his inheritance and was helped in shouldering the burden of his new responsibilities by his younger brother, until he chose as his wife Lady Constance, the daughter of a neighbouring nobleman.

Less than a year later Roger, now aged forty, followed the example of his brother and was himself married. His bride, Eleanor, was only half his age, but their devotion to each other was plain to see.

"Father."

Sir Richard's recollections of bygone days were brought to an abrupt end. He had been so deeply engrossed in his memories that Felicity had come in without his hearing or seeing her.

"My dear child," he murmured, turning to her with a smile. "I did not realise you had come in. Forgive me. I was just thinking about... Well, just thinking."

"Sleeping too I think, dear father."

"Maybe. " He smiled fondly at her. "I am getting old."

"Nonsense! Besides, there's no harm in your taking a little nap in the afternoon. It's such a warm day too. Just look at that sunshine. But I must speak with you, Father," she went on, suddenly serious.

"What is it, my dear? Is something troubling you?"

"Yes."

"Well, tell me all about it. Perhaps I can help you."

"Father, I fear you may not be pleased by what I have to say."

"Tell me anyway, and I shall decide. Come, sit beside me and tell me what is troubling you."

Felicity came over and sat herself down beside Sir Roger. Then nervously, she took his hand in her own and began.

"Father, I am in love." She stopped, embarrassed, and looked for the half-expected disappointing reaction. But Sir Roger merely smiled, gently released his hand and stroked Felicity's cheek.

"I know, my dear child," he said softly. "I know." He went on, looking at her steadily and with love. "I've seen the two of you together when you thought no one could see you. I have seen the way he looks at you, and the way you look at him. I see….true love."

"And you are not angry?"

"Angry? Oh no, my dearest, I am not. How could I be angry with you? How could I make you unhappy? No. Martin is a good man, and I think very highly of him. I can well understand your falling in love with him."

"But he is only your steward, Father. He has no noble blood in him. He is only a servant, and I am the daughter of the Lord of the Manor."

"Through the death of my brother I am, as you say, the Lord of the Manor" he replied. "But does that make me a better man, a better human being, than my steward?"

"You think well of him, don't you Father?"

"I think he is an honourable man. He is, to my certain knowledge, hardworking and intelligent. He is responsible, reliable and conscientious. I do not think that any reasonable woman would need to feel ashamed to be his wife."

"Father… Oh, my dear, dear Father! I am so happy to hear you say such things about the man I love. May I have your blessing and permission to see him?"

"That would be most irregular," replied Sir Roger in tones of mock severity that caused Felicity to shrink back and tears start to her eyes.

Did the dear child imagine, he mused, that he was unaware that she was already 'seeing' Martin?

"But…" he went on. "Irregular though it be, I cannot in all conscience find any argument, moral or practical, to go against your wishes. I am an old man, and I do not wish to make my last years unhappy by seeing you wretched. Now, if you had fallen in love with some spendthrift, or ne'er-do-well, or adventurer who was after my money" -or, he thought, someone such as the waster I was once – "I would be speaking to you in very different terms. But I trust Martin, and I will not stand in your way."

Felicity gave him a hug of affection and, throwing her arms round his neck, planted a kiss on his forehead. Then she ran from the room to go and find her lover.

That very night, Sir Roger suffered a heart attack. It turned out fortunately to be mild enough for him to be up and about again in a matter of a few days, but he was severely shaken by the attack and moved far less freely than before. He had now to rely on a walking stick to help him get about. He recovered slowly, but never regained his former vigour.

Meanwhile, the friendship between Felicity and Martin developed, and in due course their wedding was announced. Sir Roger, feeling old and sensing that his death was not far off, had been engaged in long and serious talks with Master Howard, his lawyer, arranging with him a generous provision for Felicity and her husband in the event of his death.

"For I tell you, Master Howard," he said, "I have no other heirs or dependents, and I feel that death is near. My only wish now is to be spared long enough by Almighty God to see Martin and Felicity happily wed. May God will it so."

God did indeed will it so. Sir Roger lived long enough not only to see the young couple married, but to see also two fine grandchildren born to them in the next three years. Then one afternoon he collapsed and fell heavily to the floor. His servants carried him over to his bed, and called for Martin and Felicity. As they bent anxiously over him, he half-opened his eyes and gestured to them to come close.

"Listen, my children," he murmured, in a voice that was little more than a whisper. "I know that I am dying, but there are two things that I must tell you before I die."

He stopped, breathed heavily and continued with an effort.

"This is a secret that I have kept to myself for many years and... that I ought... to have... confessed to you..."

"Confessed? What have you to confess, Father?"

"My child... Listen... Martin... I have always had a high regard for you... I have always watched to see... that you never wanted for anything... That if ever I could help you I would always do so... I have tried to be like a... like a ...." His voice trailed off.

"You have been as a father to me," Martin assured him.

"That is because... because..." his voice faded again.

"Because what?"

"Because you are... my son."

Martin and Felicity looked at each other aghast. The old man surely, could not mean this. He went on, struggling to find breath, and with his voice scarcely audible as they bent low over him to catch his words.

"When I came back... to England... from the Holy Land, I made up my mind... to lead a better life than I had led before. And... I believe... that I did so. But on the night of my return, I unfortunately fell in with a group of my old friends... Friends whom I had not seen for ten years or more." He paused, fighting to get his breath. "To put it briefly, they persuaded me... to celebrate my safe return to them... in proper style. We... went to... the tavern...To my shame, I got myself drunk, for the very last time... There was one very pretty wench... very pretty... One I had been fond of once... before, and..."

He fell silent again, and his eyes filled with tears.

"Don't say any more. We understand. Just rest."

"No. I am going... The second... secret... is about... you, Felissss..."

His voice died away into silence and, as they gazed on his impassive face, he passed away.

The horror of the secret that Sir Roger had disclosed had sunk in. Felicity and Martin could only stare at each other in utter dismay. If Martin really was the son of Sir Roger, then they were brother and sister as well as husband and wife.

I have married my own sister, thought Martin.

I have married my own brother, thought Felicity.

What were they to do? Were they to say nothing, seeing that they alone presumably knew this awful truth? But that was not possible; how could they possibly continue to live together knowing the truth? And then there were their two children, who complicated an already fraught situation. Perhaps they should consult the priest, though each knew that they had both committed, even though unwittingly, a sin that the church could never forgive. Should Felicity go away and take the children with her? Should Martin leave? This would mean heartbreak for both, and would still leave a terrible burden of guilt. That evening they plumbed the depths of misery, and were utterly unable to console each other. For three days they could hardly manage to speak to each other.

According to the terms of Sir Roger's will, Martin had inherited the Manor House. His old place of work was to become his home. It gave him no joy however, and many times he caught himself wishing he had never met Felicity. Yet he could not stop loving her and wanting to be with her. He would have to make some arrangements for her if they were obliged to separate, since Sir Roger had made everything over to Martin, knowing that Felicity, as Martin's wife, would be well cared for. The mere thought of having to give consideration to such arrangements made Martin angry and confused; he could not think of Felicity as anything other than his dear wife, whom it was his duty to love and cherish and keep.

On the evening of the third day Martin was sitting dejectedly on a stone bench in the garden, delaying as long as possible the moment when he would have to go indoors for, try as he might, he had still not been able to think of any words of comfort to say to Felicity. As for her, she was in the nursery, trying to distract herself from her misery by amusing the children. A servant found them both and told them that an old woman had come to the Manor who had important news that concerned both of them. They made their separate ways to the drawing room to meet her.

"When I heard that Sir Roger had died," the old woman began by way of introduction, "I knew I had to come to you. For more than twenty years now I have kept a secret that -"

"A secret!" exclaimed Martin. "Another one. What more misery can this one bring?"

"Aye, a secret," replied the old lady calmly. "You see, I used to be the nurse in the household of Sir Richard. He was the brother of Sir Roger and your uncle. The same Roger that used to be called 'Roger the Reckless', but who changed his ways after he came back from the Crusades."

"I do not imagine," said Felicity, "that you can tell me anything new about Roger the Reckless who became Sir Roger. He was my father."

"No, my dear. He was not your father."

"Not my father? What do you mean?"

"You, my dear child, are the daughter of Sir Roger's brother, Sir Richard. But I was pledged to secrecy about you, and I am only able to tell you now because Sir Roger, your uncle, made me swear to say nothing as long as he was alive."

The death of Sir Roger had left the old nurse finally able to reveal the true facts of Felicity's birth, facts known to nobody else. Although Felicity had always imagined herself to be Roger's daughter, she was in truth, as the old woman had said, his niece. Her true father, Richard, had died just two days before she was born. He had been thrown from his horse and killed while out riding. The shock of this tragedy had proved fatal to both Lady Constance and her baby, a little girl who was born prematurely and died within minutes of coming into the world. In the midst of all the grieving, another baby girl was born; one of Lady Constance's maids was delivered of a healthy girl, but died herself in giving birth. The poor girl had been afraid to tell anyone who was the father of the child, but Lady Constance, supported by her husband, had taken her in and looked after her when her condition became obvious. Now the poor baby, orphaned and deprived of the kindly presence of her aristocratic protectors, was left helpless and alone in the world, with no one to care for her save her devoted nurse. The only people to know who was the father of this poor orphan girl were the nurse, Sir Richard himself and his brother Roger, to whom Richard had earlier confided his guilt. Sir Richard had never felt that any useful purpose would be served if he were to tell Lady Constance that it was he who had fathered the illegitimate child. Even Roger had only a sketchy understanding of the circumstances of the baby's conception, which would have surprised anyone who knew the kind of person Sir Richard was. Nevertheless, Roger and Eleanor could not see the poor infant left destitute, and so they had had no hesitation in taking the orphan into their own home and family, and bringing her up as their own daughter. Eleanor, as it turned out, was to prove unable to give Sir Roger a son or daughter of his own, and for this reason if for no other, Felicity was especially dear to both of them. They both wished to keep their adopted daughter in ignorance of the truth concerning her birth for as long as possible; ideally, she would never know.

But then the fever had carried off his dear Eleanor, and Sir Roger, who was to grieve for her to his dying day, had begun to think that Felicity perhaps had a right to know that she was not his daughter. Perhaps. Or perhaps it would not be kind to unsettle her by giving her such startling news. So he had said nothing and had died in a vain attempt to tell her, at the very last minute, with his dying breath.

As the old nurse concluded her story, Martin and Felicity felt as though a great black cloud that had been hanging over them had been blown out of the sky, letting the bright sunshine stream in. They rushed into each other's arms and hugged and wept for sheer joy. They were not siblings after all, but cousins. Everything was all right.

"Some surprisingly naughty goings-on there, my love," commented Jessie. "But I am pleased it had a happy ending."

"Just like a Haydn trio," observed Traffy. "Now, how about some Beethoven?"

The Cup Final

"Sorry I can't make it for Friday next week," said Traffy.

They had just come to the end of an exhausting afternoon's playing, during which the chief sufferers had been two of Haydn's Piano trios and one of Schubert's.

"Beethoven next time, I think," announced Velly. "Are we agreed?"

They were, and now tired but happy, they were trying to arrange their next meeting.

"What about Thursday?" asked Velly.

"Sorry, no can do," apologised Pickle.

"I can manage Saturday afternoon if that's any help," offered Traffy.

"Saturday afternoon? This Saturday afternoon?" returned Pickle with some spirit, and in a tone of voice that implied that Traffy had suggested they might all have a shot at playing Mozart or Mendelssohn on a kazoo, or a comb and tissue-paper. "Traffy, my son, are you not aware that this coming Saturday is the day of the Cup Final? I'm not, definitely not, going to miss that."

Traffy recoiled in mock terror, and played a slow descending minor arpeggio.

"I didn't know you were a footer fan," said Velly.

"Oh yes. Mind you, I was never any great shakes as a player. But I have always followed the game, and I never miss watching the Cup Final. Not even for Beethoven. He'll have to wait, bless him."

Jessie, who had come in to warn the trio that it was getting rather near teatime and she was wondering if they intended to play for much longer, found Pickle's attitude amusing.

"My word," she said. "You do sound serious about it, Pickle. I hope to goodness your TV set doesn't throw a wobbler, or you don't find yourself stuck with guests arriving unexpectedly."

"Well, I've not missed one in the last twenty years or more," Pickle replied with a laugh. "It's just something I really enjoy every year. Big occasion and all that, you know."

"Anyway," said Velly, calling the meeting to order. "To return to our muttons, as the French say. Shall we leave it until Monday week then? That may just give Pickle time to recover in the event of his team's losing."

Monday week suited both Traffy and Pickle as it happened, so that was agreed on.

Traffy, who had sat quietly at the piano while the others tidied away their instruments, suddenly said, "Talking of the Cup Final reminds me of a sad case, rather like Pickle's."

"How do you mean?" queried Pickle.

"Well, there was this young lad who was mad on football and was desperate to watch the Cup Final on TV. There was no reason, apparently, why anything should occur to prevent him from doing so, but..."

"But what?"

"Something did, I'm afraid."

"Is there a story here?" asked Velly suspiciously.

"It's not sad, is it?" Jessie wanted to know. "It sounds as if it must be."

"It's a bit sad, I suppose, but fate has a big hand in it – or coincidence, if you like."

"It'll have to wait till next Monday, though," Velly stated, having guessed why Jessie had joined them. "There isn't time now. But it's good to know there's a story ready and waiting for when we next meet."

So the friends parted.

The following Monday week, with the Cup Final safely behind them, the three began with a quick run-through of another of Haydn's trios, ready to tackle some serious Beethoven. But first, Traffy had to tell his tale of a previous Cup Final.

Peter Mallener selected a nice ripe apple from the fruit bowl on the sideboard and settled himself comfortably on the settee next to his young brother, in front of the TV set. He leaned back with a contented "Aah!" as they watched the lengthy build-up to the Cup Final, the interviews with the fans of the two teams, the predictions, the profiles of various players, the discussions with the experts and ex-players, all of which would go on for the next hour until the match proper would begin.

"At least I'm not going to miss it this year," he declared. "Remember last year's fiasco?"

"Yes. When Grandma and Grandad came round just after the kick-off."

"And we had to do those 'little' jobs for them that ended up taking ages."

"But we did at least see the video later that evening," young John reminded Peter.

"It's not the same though as seeing it live as it actually happens. By the evening it's just... well, history. And we knew the result by then. No, I've set my heart on seeing the real thing this year. And nothing's going to stop me."

"There's no reason why anything, or anybody, should, is there?" replied John. "Relax."

It was at this moment that their mother came into the sitting room in a state of some agitation.

"Can one of you please just pop round to Auntie Jo's with some books?" she pleaded. "You'll only be away ten minutes, and I can't go myself because I'm up to my eyes in the kitchen. And your Dad's gone off to his cricket."

"Oh, mum," moaned Peter. "It's the Cup Final. You know what Auntie Jo's like. She'll keep us talking all afternoon, and we'll miss the match."

"No she won't, dear. She'll be expecting you because I've just phoned her, and I made a point of telling her you wouldn't want to be kept away from watching the match. So you'll only have to give her the books and come away again straight away. She needs the books for this afternoon, otherwise you could have gone later."

"All right," Peter agreed, reluctantly, rising from the depths of the settee. "Where are the books?"

"Thank you so much, dear," said Mrs Mallener, relieved. "They're out here."

"There's still loads of time before kick-off," John informed him. "You'll be back in plenty of time. And," he added mischievously, "I don't mind finishing your apple for you – in case you're not back before midnight."

Nellie O'Brien, a widow in her late seventies, had been aware for some time that there was a worn patch in the carpet by the door between her living room and the kitchen. It was the most heavily used piece of carpet in the house but Nellie, who wasn't too well off, had kept putting off the moment when she would have to replace the carpet. Her son Sean, a lorry driver, had driven over to see her one day, and had pointed out to Nellie that the wear on the carpet was becoming serious, if not positively dangerous. There would, he warned her, be an accident soon if she didn't replace at least the worn section. Nellie agreed and her son, striking while the iron was hot, had driven Nellie to town, where he had helped her to choose a new carpet. The following day, the carpet dealer had come to measure up. He assured her that the new carpet would be delivered and the fitter would come and lay it in four days time. Nellie, who had been worried about the condition of the carpet, was pleased to have at last done something about it, and her son went away at the end of his brief visit relieved that a potential hazard to his mother's well-being had been attended to.

Unfortunately, as it turned out, the carpet fitter telephoned Nellie on the morning he was due and informed her that he was unable to come that day, after all. He would however be there first thing next morning. He was very sorry, he said, at the inconvenience he was causing.

Some forty miles away, young Peter Mallener was also to have cause to regret the carpet fitter's re-arrangement of his schedule.

It was an ironical and sad twist of Fate that decreed that on the afternoon of the day when her new carpet should have been fitted, Sean O'Brien's prophecy was to come true – old Mrs. O'Brien had the misfortune to trip over the hole in her carpet and suffer a bad fall. A neighbour fortunately heard her calls for help, and within an hour she was in a hospital bed, badly bruised and badly shaken, and with a broken arm.

Cathy Lodge decided that she did not after all need to call on her friend Liz – she would do her bit of shopping first, and perhaps drive round to Liz's house afterwards. Her main concern for the moment was to find a parking space that was not too far from the row of shops. She decided to try along Acacia Avenue, and she was in luck. There, just outside No. 42, was a vacant space. Delighted at her unexpected good fortune, Cathy parked her little red Mini, locked it, and made for the shops. She was in no hurry; the car was safely and handily parked, so she could take her time over her purchases.

Young Bert Simpson had only been used to driving Davidson and Co's small delivery vans, but the boss, Mr Davidson himself, had insisted that Bert should make this important delivery; an important contract was at stake, and he was extremely anxious not to lose this business. It was of course most unfortunate that Sean O'Brien, who would normally have made this delivery, had had to drive over to see his mother in hospital some forty miles away. Since there were no other drivers free to drive Sean's lorry, Bert had, with no great enthusiasm, agreed to do this job for Mr Davidson. Sean's lorry was far bigger than the little van he was familiar with, and Bert was definitely nervous behind the wheel of the 'big beast' as he called it...

All went well, however, and Bert was beginning to get the hang of the big beast along the open road. But nearer to town, driving was less straightforward. There were traffic lights, hill starts, tight corners, and various other reminders for Bert that this lorry was a very different proposition from the little van. The crunch came as he drove along Acacia Avenue. A small child, accompanied by an excited dog, came running out of a garden in laughing pursuit of a tennis ball. Bert, already nervous enough, saw the danger in time to avoid hitting the child, but in his frantic efforts to control the heavy vehicle, drove it onto the pavement and crashed into the wall of No. 42, demolishing a large section of it.

The wording on the side of the van read 'Michael O'Flaherty, Building Contractor', but the man himself was always known as Mickie the Brickie or, more likely, Mick the Brick. Mr O'Flaherty was happy with either. He had spent most of the morning tidying up the mess left behind when Bert Simpson had driven his lorry into the wall of No. 42 Acacia Avenue, where Peter Mallener's aunt Jo lived. Having cleared the site and inspected the foundations of the wall to make sure that they did not need to be re-laid, he finally unloaded a supply of bricks from his van, leaving them in neat piles on the front path of the house. He then went off for a late-ish snack lunch. Now he was intending to make an immediate start on laying the bricks for the new wall. He arrived back in Acacia Avenue just in time to see a red Mini drive into the vacant parking space outside No. 42 where his van had been conveniently parked all morning.

"Drat the woman!" muttered Mick, as he drove on past the Mini and watched Cathy set off for the shops.

Typical, thought Mick. Just as he was looking forward to knocking off early after laying a row or two of bricks, and going home to watch the Cup Final at three. He wanted to be away quickly and not have to waste time searching for somewhere to park his van. Mick was, in fact, only having to come out on this day because his mate, who was to have done this particular job, had been taken ill. At least he could listen to the radio commentary. But first he had to park the van, so he drove on, searching for a space. Unfortunately, as it was a Saturday afternoon, the Avenue was full of parked cars, and there was no other space anywhere in the immediate vicinity. So Mick had no choice but to drive round until he could find somewhere free. He noticed, however, as he drove past No. 42, that the bricks were still where he had left them, in neat little piles just inside the gateway, well hidden by a privet hedge that ran alongside where the new wall would stand.

Jeff Hamley, Peter Mallener's friend, was hurrying home on his bike along Acacia Avenue, anxious not to miss the kick-off. He sped past No. 42 just as Peter was arriving to deliver his mother's books to Auntie Jo.

"Hi Peter!" he called out. "Can't stop! Don't want to miss the start! Cheerio!"

And he was off. Peter turned to call out a cheery greeting to the departing cyclist. In doing so, he failed to notice the bricks that Mick had left behind. In his haste, he tripped over them, lurched awkwardly against the gatepost and fell to the ground, landing heavily on the arm that clutched the precious books. He heard the crack as he hit the ground and broke his arm.

Mick, having finally parked his van not too far away, arrived on the spot within minutes of the accident. He quickly informed Peter's aunt, and in a short time the ambulance was on its way to Acacia Avenue.

But by then, of course, the Cup Final had already started. Once again Peter was obliged to watch a recording of the match instead of seeing it live.

"Poor lad!" commented Jessie. "Talk about adding insult to injury. He must have been as sick as a parrot."

The three men looked at Jessie.

"Where on earth did you pick up that expression?" asked her husband.

"I suppose it must have been on the telly," Jessie replied, somewhat taken aback by their reaction to her use of that particular image. "I say, it's not rude or anything, is it?" she asked, anxiously.

"Of course not," laughed Pickle. "It's just that it sounds so odd coming from you. There's no reason why you shouldn't use it. In fact, speaking personally, I'm over the moon about it."

To Jessie's mystification, the three men burst into childish laughter.

"Time for Beethoven, I think," said Velly at last.

The Two Crusaders

Traffy was having problems with some awkward phrasing in the trio that they were playing.

"Let's take it from bar 58 again," suggested Pickle. "We'll do it a fair bit slower too."

They tried it again more slowly, but it didn't seem to help much. Traffy continued to struggle. Finally he studied the score and worked out a different fingering.

"It's that little figure here," he said, pointing it out to the others. "That awkward jump, just after the change of key. You know, it reminds me of a very similar passage that I always had trouble with in Weber's 'Konzerstuck'. I used to play that when I was younger," he added with a touch of pride.

"Now that's a piece we ought to hear more often," commented Pickle. "There's so much colour and light and... sheer sparkle: very medieval in spirit, even if it's so very early nineteenth century in its style and its rich orchestration. I've always thought the story behind it very evocative," he went on. "Especially the moment when the lady has a vision telling her that her crusader husband has been killed in battle, and she faints and is woken from her swoon by the distant sound of the horn –"

"– which announces the return of the knight, alive and well, at the head of his followers?" suggested Velly.

"Naturally. Oddly enough," Pickle went on, "about a year ago I read a story that's very similar to that Konzerstuck story. It's based on the crusades and the return of the knight to his lady."

"Let's just get this little problem sorted out," suggested Traffy. "I think I can see what I need to do. Then Pickle can tell us his gothic tale."

"And I'll fetch Jessie, so that –"

"Jessie's here already," announced that lady, pushing open the door and entering with a tray of refreshments. "It must be almost storytime, surely?"

"Give us five more minutes."

"Right you are. I'll sit quietly like a good girl. Then I'll pour the tea, and we can all listen to a good story. Whose turn is it today?"

Pickle put down his cup and cleared his throat. "It's about two crusaders," he said, for Jessie's benefit.

Big Aedwin stared down at the rush-strewn floor of his hut. He was a tall, well-built young man, immensely strong – as he needed to be to wield the big axe with which he felled the sturdy oaks in the forest that formed part of Sir Robert's estate. There was much building going on, and the serfs were kept busy in the forest, in addition to tending their strips of cultivation. It was a warm summer evening, and Aedwin sprawled against the wooden wall of the hut, relaxing his thick muscular arms and massive thighs. Now and then he flexed his muscles to prevent them from stiffening up after the exertions of the day. Then he would stretch, and feel the strength coursing through his powerful body.

Unfortunately, Aedwin, was less strong of will than of physique. He had a weakness for drink, a weakness that he bitterly regretted, and in his sober moments he would curse his inability to master it. The tragedy of that was that it threatened to ruin his relationship with Alice, with whom he was in love and who had declared that she returned his affection.

"Now look you, Aedwin," she had said to him only the previous week, "I will have nothing to do with a man who cannot control –"

"Trust me, my sweet. I will overcome it. I swear it, for the sake of your dear love," Aedwin had answered her earnestly.

"You know that Sir Robert has said that he will place no obstacle in the way of our getting married, and I will gladly be your bride. But I make this one condition – I will not wed with any man who is the slave of drink. If you can keep from letting strong liquor pass your lips twixt now and this day next year, then I shall be yours, I promise, and proud to be so."

She smiled, encouraging him, for she was very devoted to the man and wished above all things to be the wife of a reformed and sober Aedwin.

The next day, Aedwin was up betimes, and spent an hour on his strip. Then he took up his axe and went off to the forest where he toiled with more energy than ever, fired by the strength of his love for Alice and by his resolve to turn over a new leaf for her sake. But the sun was hot, the day was long, and the woodcutter's work arduous. So that when it was time to stop, he made his way, soaked in perspiration and aching with a healthy fatigue back to his hut. He heard his friends calling to him to join them at Majorie's ale-house, but his Alice was always present in his thoughts and he remained deaf to their repeated invitations. So now he sat alone, tortured by thirst. The dear girl was right, of course. It was a cause for shame that a strapping giant of a man like him should be the slave of such a demeaning weakness. His gaze fell on his great powerful hands; here was a permanent reminder if he needed one of the folly of his frailty, for he had lost the top joint of his little finger as the consequence of an accident he had had when using his axe while incapable through drink. Again he swore that with God's help he would master his weakness and show himself worthy of his Alice's love. But his throat felt very dry, and visions of a flagon of ale floated temptingly before him. Perhaps, just one cup at Majorie's, and then... But as he sat there arguing with himself, a prey to conflicting desires, a shadow fell across the doorway, blocking out the ray of the setting sun. Aedwin looked up and saw before him a man in a long black gown.

"Good evening, Holy Father," Aedwin greeted him, and stood up awkwardly. "Come inside. You are welcome in my humble home."

The priest stepped into the hut. He was an itinerant preacher and needed to reach his destination before dark, so he wasted no time in preliminaries.

"I come not to preach the Holy Gospel, nor to beg alms, but to find men. Men such as you, my son."

Aedwin frowned, uncomprehending. The priest went on.

"I have been sent by Peter the Hermit himself. This Peter is a holy man with a great vision. Just as your lord, Sir Robert, is about to set off for the Holy Land to fight for the glory of the Christian Church, so Peter the Hermit is organising a march to be undertaken by the common people."

"The Holy Land? Is this the great matter that men call the Crusade?"

"The Crusade you speak of is for knights and nobles and men of high degree, that have money and can raise armies of soldiers with horses and arms," the priest explained. "Peter the Hermit has a vision of the common people also marching to the Holy Land. God has need of people of low station too, you see. He seeks people of your sort, my son. You would, I am sure, make a doughty warrior for Christ."

Aedwin sat silent, thinking, as the priest took up his talk.

"There are many, many pilgrims – brave, God-fearing Christian souls – who go on their pilgrimages to visit the holy shrines, but who are attacked and robbed and killed by the heathen Turks. The Pope himself is most distressed at this unholy massacre of innocent Christian folks, and at the great council in France he has called upon all who believe to take part in this great enterprise, to free Jerusalem from the stranglehold of the infidel."

Aedwin seemed to stir himself out of his reverie.

"Is the Holy Land far distant, Father?"

"It lies beyond the seas. But large numbers of good sturdy men, just like you, have, by God's good grace, responded to the call to swell the numbers of those who wish to undertake this great mission."

The priest tarried only a short while, telling Aedwin as much as he could of the great popular Crusade that had been initiated by men such as Peter the Hermit and Walter the Penniless, but he departed without having secured any firm commitment from the big woodcutter, who pensively watched the black-clad figure melt into the enveloping darkness as he went on his way.

Left alone, Aedwin had much to reflect on. Had he not

sworn that with God's help he would conquer his weakness? Maybe God was now giving him a means of removing himself from all such temptation. Surely it was a great work for God, this Crusade?

But how could he leave his work, with the demand for building wood so great at present? Above all, how could he leave his Alice?

Aedwin slept a troubled sleep that night.

The next morning, as he and his neighbours laboured in the forest, they saw coming along the path a procession of mounted men. The horses were brightly caparisoned, and their riders wore armour and were equipped with swords, lances and shields. The Lord of the Manor, Sir Robert, was off with his retainers to the Holy Land; they were members of the great army that would do battle with the Saracens in what was to become the First Crusade. As the splendid cavalcade passed slowly but purposefully by, the woodmen paused in their work to stare. Envy and admiration vied for supremacy in the mind of big Aedwin as he gazed after the disappearing figures.

Meanwhile, from her window in the Manor, the Lady Eleanore was also watching the procession as it gradually passed out of sight over the fields, and fighting in vain to keep back her tears. Unlike many knights, Sir Robert was a God-fearing man, and his sole motive for undertaking the Crusade was to see the Holy Land restored to Christian rule, so that pilgrims might go unmolested and in safety to the Holy City.

Sir Robert had no qualms about absenting himself from his manor; he knew that the Church would protect it, along with his lands, until he should return. Of course, he regretted bitterly the need to leave his wife and two young children behind, but he preferred to do that rather than expose them to the risks and dangers that he knew he himself would have to face. Besides, he had complete faith in his steward, Simon, to ensure that his affairs were kept in good order, and his family protected.

Sir Robert's word was law, and whatever she might have felt in her heart, Lady Eleanore was obliged to accept the decisions her husband made for her. Would she ever see him again? She knew that she had no power, no right, to keep him from going on his dangerous campaign. Proudly she had kept back her tears until Sir Robert had left her, but now that he was gone, she gave full vent to her grief.

By the end of the day, Aedwin had come to a decision. Without saying a word to anyone, not even to Alice who might have dissuaded him, he slipped away, unseen, to begin the long and treacherous journey that would take him across Europe and beyond. He would become a recruit in Peter the Hermit's army of ill-equipped and untrained volunteers, answering God's call to the People's Crusade.

Simon, the steward of Sir Robert, was feeling pleased with himself. He had never before been so aware of his own importance, had never had to exercise responsibility for such a lengthy period. He had always proved competent and reliable in all small matters and he knew that his master trusted him implicitly, but he was enjoying being in charge in his lord's extended absence. It was now a good three years since Sir Robert had departed for Jerusalem, leaving him to oversee the manor and its lands. Proudly, he mounted his horse and set off to cast a proprietary eye over various parts of the land attached to the manor, hoping as he set off to find some way of asserting his authority over the serfs in his charge.

As it happened, Alice has set out the same morning to gather berries in the wood, and was making her way back to her cottage when she saw the steward himself riding towards he along the track. As she stepped aside to allow him to pass, he reined in his horse and addressed her.

"Good morning, Alice. What are you doing abroad this fine sunny morning?"

"If you please, sir, I have been out gathering berries for my kitchen," she replied.

She has a pretty face, he thought, wondering why he had not really noticed her peasant beauty before. He stared proudly down at her, admiring the way in which the sunlight gilded her auburn hair which had escaped from the snood on her head while she worked. Dismounting, he offered to escort her back. She was touched by his gallantry, though overawed at finding herself spoken to in so friendly a way by one whose station was so far above her own. She felt even more uncomfortable when, in reply to his clever questioning, she heard herself telling him that, though promised to Aedwin the woodcutter, she had begun to despair of seeing him again.

"But," she informed Simon, "If he returns, we are to be wed. Sir Robert has given his blessing to our union."

"And when will you Aedwin return, eh?" he asked, with an unpleasant smile. "I think you will not be seeing him this day, my pretty maid."

With these words he led her firmly through the doorway, scattering the hens that clucked and pecked at the floor.

"Come," he said. "You'll not refuse my love, I know."

Alice hesitated, still uncertain as to the meaning of his words. It still puzzled her that Simon, the steward of Sir Robert himself, could talk to her of his love; she was beneath his notice, surely? But he was fingering the stray wisps of hair that fell across her face, and as she looked into his eyes she could no longer put off the awful realisation that it was his intention to make love to her, there on the earthen floor. His fingers moved down over her throat, and then, with a sudden movement, he ripped away the front of her gown. Covering her lips with his own and seizing her wrists, he easily mastered her frantic struggles to free herself from his grasp. All she could do now was to resign herself to her fate, her eyes opening wide in panic. She lay there, limp and finally unresisting, as he took her.

Afterwards, sated, he stood up and, without saying another word, strode out of the doorway, leaving her distressed and sobbing as he rode triumphantly back to the Manor. After all, what did it mean to be steward if one could not enjoy certain privileges bestowed by rank?

Lady Eleanore grew daily more pale, and was almost inconsolable as the days passed and no news arrived of Sir

Robert. Their two children brought her some comfort, it was true, but little Blanche was too young to understand why her father was never there to talk to her and amuse her in play. As for Master Thomas, he was if anything a little scornful of his mother's tears, and was looking forward to the time when he should be old enough to join his father in the great Crusade.

Then for Alice, there came a terrible discovery; she realised that she was with child. Here was a new and frightening situation. How could she face the women with their gossip, when her condition became obvious, she who was promised to Aedwin who was away somewhere? What if Aedwin were suddenly to return and find her expecting a child by another man, after having sworn to be his? She felt dirty, disgraced and utterly desolate. Was it not bad enough to have lost her beloved Aedwin, who had gone away without a word, without having this second awful disaster befall her? The poor girl even reproached herself as being responsible for his decision to leave her; maybe she had spoken too harshly to him, expected too much of him. She could see no way of living with his new misfortune, and saw nothing to bring her even the smallest crumb of comfort. What had she now to live for, with not even a certain hope that Aedwin might some day come back to her, forgive her and take her back, sullied as she was?

It was at this time also that Lady Eleanore had a dream. She had fallen asleep in the solar in the warm autumn sunshine, and a vivid dream had come to her in which she saw, with horrifying clarity, Sir Robert lying dead on the battlefield. The vividness of the dream caused her to wake up with a violent scream. Her women came running to attend her. She told them of the dream, and in deep distress, collapsed fainting on a chair. Her panicking women feared for her life and ran hither and thither, searching in the kitchens and the various chests for herbs and medicines with which to revive her. It was all to no avail; she just lay there, pale as death.

Suddenly the sound of a horn was heard, echoing across the fields. The women, ceasing their frantic ministrations, ran to the window. They saw a great cloud of dust, raised by a troop of men and horses approaching the Manor. There was a clatter of hooves, the jingle of harnesses, the gleam of metal, the murmur of voices coming ever nearer. Gradually it dawned on the watching women that this was Sir Robert himself returning from the Holy Land. Their excitement mounting, they redoubled their efforts to revive Lady Eleanore, but it was not until Sir Robert himself strode into the room and took her up in his arms that his wife finally came out of her swoon. There was a joyous reunion, and celebrations were speedily organised. There was singing, dancing, drinking, eating and merrymaking unrestrained at the Manor, as all celebrated the return of its Lord.

Alice knew nothing of these festivities. Unable to face an unutterably bleak future, she had taken her own life, and her bloated body went floating slowly, face down, in the river. It bumped against the arch of the bridge and came to rest there, wedged against the stonework.

Whatever glory or glamour Aedwin had imagined he might enjoy in the People's Crusade had turned sour. The reality of the march was a harsh and cruel one, making terrible physical demands upon the thousands of poor wretches who struggled on, buoyed up only by a naïve acceptance that all the hardship and misery were to be endured because it was God's work that was being done, by the exhortations of the leaders who somehow managed to inspire a sense of unity and purpose in a doomed and pathetic rabble of ill-equipped, hopelessly innocent and trusting rustics. Time after time, their lives were put at risk. Ambushes, open hostility, exhaustion and disease all took their toll. Men died by the hundred. Yet there were always, it seemed, plenty more to take their places and even swell the numbers of those persevering as the long and weary march dragged on. Finally, in utter desperation and completely demoralised, Aedwin and a small band of men who had shared his hardships decided to turn back and attempt to find their way home again. By sheer good fortune, Aedwin had eventually fallen in with Sir Robert's party of soldiers, and had followed in their wake. So it was that Aedwin found himself among those who had been with Sir Robert to share in the triumph of his return.

Aedwin's first concern, however, was not for the feasting or the dancing or the merrymaking; nor was it for the drinking. Throughout the appalling privations of the march, he had been sustained not only by his strong constitution, but also by the thought of seeing his cherished Alice once again. It was to her cottage by the river that he now made his way.

It was Aedwin himself who found her body by the bridge. He had come back too late for her to see him safely returned; too late to tell her that they could now be made man and wife, because he had faithfully kept the promise he had made to her immediately before his departure.

"Not quite the happy ending that Weber gave us," said Traffy. "But a riveting tale all the same."

"The common touch," said Velly. "It wasn't all about knights in shining armour and swooning aristocratic ladies."

"Rotten luck for poor old Aedwin, though. No reward for him for conquering his demons, and being so loyal."

"Talking of conquering demons..." countered Traffy. "Suppose we have another last go at that presto, just to make sure I've mastered it did for good."

The Lord of the Spirits

"My niece is coming to see us next week," Velly announced to the others, as they prepared to a session of music making.

"The married one?" enquired Traffy.

"Yes. She's quite a good pianist. Almost..." – and he stressed the word as he turned with a broad smile to Traffy – "Almost as talented as you are, old son."

Traffy smiled at the compliment, but limited it to a cheery, "I don't suppose she's half my age?"

"She's probably around twenty five, I'd say," Velly volunteered vaguely. "I'm hopeless at remembering the ages of my relations. Anyway, she's bringing her husband along this time."

"Is he by any chance a musician?" inquired Pickle.

"He plays the violin, doesn't he love?" asked Jessie.

"No, that was the other chap. Steve. Tom plays the viola."

"I say, that's interesting. How good is he?"

"Pretty fair, I believe. I've only met him a few times. He's a good lad, though, and just right for Rachel."

"As the other chap – the violinist – presumably wasn't?"

"Oh, I don't know about that. Rachel was very keen on both of them at one point. In fact she could have chosen either of them, but Steve was quite suddenly moved down to the Isle of Wight with his job, which made it easier for her to decide that Tom was the right choice for her."

There was a moment's silence, then Pickle, having finished turning his violin, said, "I hope your nephew bring his viola when they come. We could do the odd piano quartet. That could be a pleasant addition to our repertory."

"I'll give 'em a call tonight," Velly assured him. "I agree with you. It would be a pleasure to –" He stopped suddenly, looking anxiously at Traffy who was sitting with a thoughtful, faraway look on his face.

"It's all right," Traffy said, emerging from his reverie. "It's this business of a girl having to choose between two chaps when she's equally fond of both of them. It reminds me of a story. The details are coming back to me."

"Say no more," ordered Velly. "Let's have another go at the Schubert, then we'll have some coffee, and after that you can regale us with your story."

"I'll be back in about an hour," said Jessie, leaving the friends to their music. "With coffee, of course," she added.

"There is," Traffy began, "a far-off land where young children, when they are naughty, are warned by their parents that if they do not behave as they should the Lord of the Spirits will come and take them away. So great is the awe in which this mysterious personage is held in the land that any child who so far forgets himself as to transgress against his parents' wishes will – if we assume that he is old enough to understand – immediately mend his ways at the mere mention of the dreaded name. Mind you, a loving mother is ill-advised to use this particular threat when her child is too young to understand..."

Many many years ago, in a country far removed from our own, lived a beautiful girl called Amina. Orphaned at an early age, she was brought up by her grandparents, who took her to live with them on their little farm on the outskirts of their tiny village nestling in the foothills of the lofty mountains. Life could be very harsh during the months of winter, but winter did not last forever and Amina's little world was a paradise on earth to her once the snows had melted and the warmth of the sun brought out the flowers, while the young birds and animals filled the air with their joyous cries. Amina would then hurry out of the farmhouse to go running and skipping over the fields, thrilled to the feel of the spring breeze in her hair or the tingle of the icy water that came tumbling down from the mountains, turning the placid streams into torrents that crashed their way over the rock-strewn river bed. All around were the valleys and hills that gladdened the heart of the young girl as she went about her duties helping her grandparents.

When she was eighteen years old, her grandmother died, and a few weeks after he had committed his dear wife's body to the earth her grandfather said to Amina, "Mina, my dear child, I am getting old, and some day I shall no longer be here to provide for you. What will you do then? You cannot manage to do all the work on the farm on your own. You are a young woman now, no longer a child, and it is time for you to choose a good husband."

"Grandfather," replied Amina, "you have always been so good and kind to me that I have never needed to look beyond these four walls. It is difficult for me to imagine life without you here to look after me. But your advice has always been sound, and what you say is right. With a husband I shall be able to manage the farm and," she added, laying her small hand on his shoulder, "I will be better able to look after you in your old age."

The old man smiled and gave a little wave of his hand as though to dismiss the last point.

"I am thinking of you and of your future," he went on. "You will have no difficulty in making a good match. There are good men here in the village – two of them in particular, either of whom I should welcome as a worthy husband for you. I think you know whom I mean?"

Amina blushed; her grandfather had spoken right.

He went on, "Janek is strong and vigorous, and I think you find him handsome?"

He looked inquiringly at her for a brief moment, and was rewarded by seeing her redden again.

"He is a hunter, who loves the woods and the fields and hills and valleys. He has a kind heart, and I know he is in love with you, for he has told me so." He paused. "And there is also Pavlo the miller. He too is young and strong and kind-hearted. He is a good worker too."

Amina looked at her wise old grandfather. Again he was right in what he said. Pavlo did indeed work hard – he had to, since he was determined to restore the fortunes of the ailing business left to him when his father hanged himself in a fit of despair.

"The mill is beginning to prosper once more," went on the old man. "I have a high regard to Pavlo. You could do worse, a lot worse, than marry him. Or Janek," he added, since he had an equal regard for both men.

Janek the hunter and Pavlo the miller had been close friends from their earliest days. Growing up together they had become inseparable companions, sharing in many a daring boyish exploit and humorous escapade. Their youthful pranks had caused momentary irritation to various of their neighbours, but there was not a trace of malice in either lad, and nobody harboured ill-will against them. Janek was the natural leader, the reckless, fearless, adventurous explorer, with a perfect foil in Pavlo, who was more thoughtful, more sensitive and imaginative, though no less brave in facing any challenge. As they grew older and more serious, their closeness had remained. Even the discovery by each of them that the other had also fallen in love with Amina was not allowed to come between them. They swore a solemn oath of loyalty, vowing that no matter which of them should prove successful in this rivalry their friendship would last till death.

At about the time of her twentieth birthday Amina finally made up her mind. She was naturally flattered and elated to know that two good men both wanted her for a wife, and she had to think very carefully before making her choice. The truth was that she was equally in love with both of them. Her choice finally fell on Janek, and they were married in the little church in the village one fine spring day, and great general rejoicing and with the heartfelt good wishes of the whole community. Everyone came to the wedding, and the joyful occasion was talked about for many days afterwards.

There was, however, one thing that only those directly concerned knew. Amina had indeed chosen Janek, but that did not stop her still being very fond of Pavlo. Nor could it make Pavlo stop loving her. Therefore, loyal to the oath he had sworn with Janek, Pavlo came to a decision. During the feasting, he sought out the bridegroom.

"Janek, my dear friend," he said. "We cannot, as you must see, always possess that which we most desire in life. I shall never cease to think of you as the best friend a man could ever have, and I do not wish to risk allowing our friendship to become spoilt by jealousy."

"Jealously? What on earth do you mean?" queried Janek, though he secretly guessed of Pavlo's thoughts. "How can jealousy come between you and me?"

"If I stay here," replied Pavlo, "I shall never be able to see Amina without being reminded of what I have lost. It would torment me to have to keep telling myself that she is another's wife. Therefore I am going away. I have some money because I have sold the mill. You alone know that. Tomorrow I shall leave the village and the new owner will come and take over the business."

"Pavlo, Pavlo, you cannot just walk out of my life this way. You cannot… You must not, simply because…"

"I must and I shall do so, my dear and most loyal friend, though it breaks my heart. Surely you can understand why I have to do this? Somebody more important than I has come to take my place in your life, by your side. Do not try to stop me, Janek. I wish you and Amina the very best that life can possibly give you. I hope and believe that you will be very happy together. I still love her, and I always shall, but she is not for me. It is a great comfort to me to know that you will make her as happy as I should have tried to do."

"Pavlo, those are the words of a true and loyal friend. If I really am obliged to bid you farewell, then I do it with a very heavy heart, for this separation is not something that I would have wished."

"I have, as I say, a bit of money," replied Pavlo. "I shall go away, over the mountains, and find work of some kind. It may be – who knows? – that I shall find new happiness in another land. Here is my hand. Let us part friends until death, as we have always been."

"Until death," returned Janek. "And beyond," he added.

The next morning, Pavlo was up before dawn, and by the time the villagers were beginning their day's work, he was well on his way on his journey over the mountains.

When Amina heard from Janek that Pavlo had severed all ties with his past, she had been both upset and incredulous. Worse she blamed herself, at least in part, for breaking up a friendship of long standing, reasoning that her decision not to marry Pavlo had had a far more devastating effect than she could have foreseen. But now two years had passed and, helped by Janek's devotion and by the need to see to the practical side of running a home, she eventually became her old self again. She also discovered that she was to have a child, and this helped to drive her thoughts in a more positive direction. Her husband and her grandfather shared her joy.

But suddenly this joy was shattered by a cruel and unexpected blow. Janek, out hunting in the neighbouring woods, was set upon by a band of brigands who brutally attacked him and left him to die. They fled, careful to leave no trace of their identity. Amina was plunged into the depths of helpless despair. How was she to cope with this new and terrible situation into which fate had thrown her? She had lost her husband, and her unborn child would be fatherless. The very word 'widow' frightened her, young as she was. She would now have to shoulder the burden of looking after her increasingly frail and dependent grandfather, as well as taking on alone the upbringing of her child. Inevitably perhaps, her thoughts turned momentarily to Pavlo, who would have been such a tower of strength to her at this time, as she confided to her grandfather.

"But, my poor child, he is far, far away. We do not even know exactly where he is. We must be strong for each other."

It was not long before rumours began to spread round the village that Pavlo had returned secretly and was responsible for Janek's death. Vicious tongues began to wag and suspicions voiced.

"Well, he went away very suddenly, without a word to

anyone, didn't he?"

"He was in love with her too – that was no secret."

"They were great friends of course, but after all, they were rivals in love, and he was the loser."

"Why should he not sneak back, do the deed, and then slip away again without showing his face?"

"Jealousy got the better of him, that's certain."

Amina and her grandfather naturally heard these malicious rumours, and they found no comfort in them.

"Grandfather, I cannot believe that Pavlo would do such a thing, can you? It was such a cowardly murder."

"No, I do not believe it. Until I see definite proof that your poor husband died at Pavlo's hands, I shall not believe him capable of such a mean act. He always wanted what was best for you." He paused. "And now that we have to think of the future. Your future. Your child's future. I say again, we must be strong for each other."

The months slipped by, and in due course Amina gave birth to a son, whom she named Janek after his father. The boy brought great happiness to the stricken household, and with the birth of a grandson the old man seemed to take on a new lease of life. Amina however, despite the pride and happiness that motherhood brought her, was less quick to regain her former serenity and remained a prey to moments of confusion and despair. At such times she would sit alone in the kitchen, weeping silent tears of bitter anguish and wondering why she was called upon to bear this burden and silently railing at the workings of an unkind Fate.

One day, leaving her grandfather sleeping in his armchair and herself feeling very low, she had gone into the kitchen to be alone with her gloomy thoughts, when she heard little Janek, by now nearly two years old, come crawling in his bustling way after her, wanting her to play with him. She turned away from him, but felt him tugging at her skirts. Again, she turned away, but he persisted, whimpering. Amina, her mind churning with all kinds of conflicting emotions, lost patience with him.

"Go away! Leave me alone!"

He started to cry, startled by the sharpness of her voice, and clung to her.

"Leave me alone, I say!" she screamed. "Do as I tell you!"

His tears and desperate need of her affection, that she was in no mood to give, made her snap.

"If you don't go away and leave me alone, I'll send for the Lord of the Spirits. Do you want him to come and take you away?"

The child was now frightened and bewildered, but his tears and cries made no impression on his poor mother, except to add to her own deep misery.

"Oh, take the child away!" she screamed.

Immediately the room was plunged in darkness, which lasted but a second. In that second however, the child had vanished. The Lord of the Spirits had taken the mother at her word.

Amina was aghast at what she had inadvertently done, and in her unbalanced state of mind she came close to doing away with herself without further thought, so complete and utterly unredeemable was her distress. She hated and despised herself for her weakness. As she saw it, she had added to the loss of her husband that of their son. How could she face life now? Slowly however, and with infinite patience, her grandfather restored her to some degree of calmness, and finally, tired by all the emotions of the day, she sank into a fitful sleep.

That night she had a dream in which she was visited by the Lord of the Spirits. He spoke to her, saying, "I have your son in my keeping. It is as you wished. Do not deny that you wished to be free of him. He's such a handsome child and now you wish to have him back, I think. Well, I will make a bargain with you. If you are ever visited by a stranger who will love you enough to marry you, and who will accept the child and bring him up as if he were his own, then the boy will be restored to you."

The dream vanished and Amina awoke. But she recalled all the details of what she had heard.

Pavlo paused with his axe resting against the block on which he had been chopping wood. He straightened his back and stretched his limbs before making a neat pile of logs in front of his hut. This was where he had come to live after departing from Janek. He had trampled for six days over the mountains and had finally settled in this village, where he had been accepted and found work as a woodcutter. His was a simple life in which working, eating and sleeping made little demand on him and in which it was rarely that anything happened to disturb his tranquil routine.

Looking up, he was aware of a strange figure coming along the track. Other villagers had also seen this stranger approaching, and upon being recognised as the wandering bard, he was quickly surrounded by a sea of eager, welcoming faces. His arrival was an event; tonight there would be storytelling, singing and talk in Big Hut. There would be gossip and news of the countryside would be passed on, for this man was an important link with the outside world. He knew all that was going on, and accompanying himself on his hand-held harp, he would sing songs of sadness, love, longing, death, victory and jealousy, as well as recounting details of everyday happenings. He was at once entertainer and carrier of news. Everyone was present that evening in Big Hut, crowding around the bard. He brought news from all the villages he had been through in the course of his travels. The people listened, eager, enthralled, to his mixture of fact and fantasy, for he also composed ballads of his own. Pavlo stood by the door, blinking in the smoky atmosphere, indifferent to the news from other parts. What interest had he in what was happening elsewhere?

Silence fell, and the bard began to intone a fresh song, one which he said he had composed himself using facts from an incident which he had been told about in a village away across the mountains. Snatches of the song came to Pavlo.

'One she chose and did him wed.
Then the other sighed and said,
Take her, loyal friend, and may

Joy be yours for many a day.
I be off, new life to find;
All that's past I leave behind.'

To Pavlo's astonishment, the song went on to set out in exact detail all the circumstances of his own departure. He began to listen more intently now. He learned more, for he discovered that Janek was dead, that he himself was suspected of killing him, that Amina had a son whom she had lost, that the child would be restored to her under certain conditions, that Amina was in deep distress and despair. As the bard finished his tale, Pavlo slipped quietly back to his hut and began to prepare himself for a long and arduous journey.

Two months had passed since baby Janek had been taken away from her, and Amina went about her duties in a listless, mechanical sort of way, always with a vague hope that some day she might see her son again. The only thing that gave her the will to carry on living, apart from the devoted love and support of her grandfather, was the thought that there might come such a change. She clung with a tenacity born of desperation to this tiny thread of hope. Each day she knelt beside the little empty bed and prayed. But the weeks passed and nothing happened. Amina began to wonder if she should ignore the promptings of the persistent instinct that told her not to lose faith. Life was beginning to seem as pointless as it had been when her husband was taken from her.

And yet there had been the dream. There was a chance.

One evening as she prayed, she heard a soft footstep in the room behind her. Recognising that it was not her grandfather's tread, she turned to see who it was that intruded. She saw an aged shepherd, wrapped in a tattered flowing cape and leaning heavily on his crook for support. His long white beard hung down over his chest, and wispy locks of white hair could be seen under his battered old hat.

"Are you praying for a miracle?" he asked.

Amina did not answer immediately. Nevertheless, it was true; she was indeed praying for a miracle. But how could this bent, raggedly dressed old man know what was tormenting her?

"I am," she whispered at length.

There was a short silence. Then the shepherd spoke again. "I am willing," he said.

"Willing to do what?" she asked, thinking he must be mad.

"I will marry you. I love you enough."

Amina recoiled in horror. He was mad. Her idea of a stranger who would come to her and bring back her son had been very different from what she now saw before her. The thought of being the wife of such a decrepit old man repelled her. She had been the wife of Janek; Janek the hunter, the strong, fearless, vigorous man she had adored. But the shepherd went on.

"And I will love your child as if he were my own flesh and blood."

These words made Amina tremble. Why was this odious man tormenting her with these words? How, outside the village, should anyone know about her child and her dream? This man was quite obviously an outsider, and yet he appeared to know everything.

"Leave me, please," she whispered. "I need to be alone."

The shepherd turned without a word, and left her. Amina knelt by the bed, and as she knelt, she had a vision. Janek stood before her. He spoke to her, telling her how he had interceded with the Lord of the Spirits, persuading him to relent so far as to give her at least a chance of recovering her son. He told her that she must marry this stranger, this unattractive shepherd, and that she would do so with his, Janek's, blessing. Janek faded from her sight, just as the shepherd walked back into the room. Amina rose and walked slowly over to him.

"I will marry you," she said.

The shepherd, in one easy movement, drew himself up to his full height and threw off his clothes and hat. Then he tore off his beard and moustache and the mop of white hair. Amina shrieked as Pavlo stood before her, and flung herself into his arms. Alarmed by her scream, her grandfather came hobbling into the room. He stopped in amazement as he saw the two lovers embracing. Then he noticed something else.

"Look," he said, and pointed towards the bed.

Little Janek lay there, sleeping peacefully.

"Ah, they didn't have radio or television, or telephones, or CDs in those days," commented Pickle. "Modern communications have taken the place of the wandering bard. The old oral tradition. Nothing recorded, or written down. Just word of mouth. And do-it-yourself entertainment, without the aid of any form of machine. Just the occasional visit from the bard to keep folks informed of the doings of the outside world, and family and friends to provide music for dancing and weddings and suchlike."

"You can't beat live music," decreed Jessie. "Now, I'd love to hear some more Schubert.

What's In A Name?

It was a fine, sunny day in June, and Velly was busy in the garden, having decided he had time to do a spot of weeding and general tidying up. But it was warm work and Velly did not wish to overdo it, so he was just beginning to wonder if it would soon be time to get up off his knees, pull off his gloves, and tidy away the trowel, secateurs and bucket. After all, what didn't get done today could wait until tomorrow. That, he reflected, was the great thing about being retired.

As if she had been reading his mind, Jessie came bustling out of the house in search of her husband.

"How much longer are you going to be, dear?" she enquired, anxiously.

"I was just thinking of calling it a day," Velly replied. "I'll come in now."

"Only, the others will be here in just over half an hour, and if you want to have a shower and get smartened up before they arrive…"

Velly assured her that he would be doing no more in the garden for now. He collected his tools together, tidied them away in the shed, and with a quick admiring glance at his handiwork, strode indoors.

When Traffy and Pickle arrived, they found Velly ready and eager for some music making.

"Would you like coffee now?" asked Jessie, having welcomed their two friends. "Or are you going to play something first?"

"Let's do a bit of Haydn to warm up with," suggested Velly. "How does that sound?"

"Suits me," Pickle assured him, and Traffy concurred.

"I'll come back in half an hour, then," said Jessie. "Maybe somebody will have a story ready by then," she added hopefully.

The Haydn trio had gone well. Velly flippantly attributed this to the fact that he had just had a shower. The others, humouring him, agreed wholeheartedly, and solemnly declared that they too would from now on make a point of having a bath before turning up for future music sessions.

"You're all as daft as one another," chuckled Jessie.

"I don't see anything wrong in having a bath," protested Pickle. "I read somewhere, a long time ago, that Bach used to enjoy bathing his children when they were small. I suspect he found it a refreshing antidote to the intellectual effort of writing fugues and inventions and so on."

"Dear old John Brook," said Traffy dreamily.

"Who's John Brook?" asked Jessie, aware that Velly was grinning away to himself, while Pickle was apparently as perplexed as she was at this mention of a newcomer.

"John Brook," repeated Traffy. "Not Charles Weaver, or Joseph Green, or Little Heathens -"

"Or Little Choirs," put in Velly.

"Or Bob Cobbler -"

"Or J.P. Branch. Or G.F. Trade."

"Hold on a minute," Pickle broke in on the stream of names being trotted out by Velly and Traffy. "Just kindly tell us who all these folks are. For a start, who's this John Brook who started it all?"

"Well," Velly explained. "It helps if you know a bit of French, or German or Italian. John Brook in German is Johann Bach. I left the Sebastian out so as not to make it too obvious."

"Very clever, I'm sure," commented Jessie, crushingly. "So, what about the other strange names you mentioned?"

Velly and Traffy, who'd played this game before, identified Weber, Verdi, Paganini, Corelli, Robert Schumann, Jean-Philippe Rameau, and Handel. Velly assured them that there were most certainly many others to be found, especially if one knew a few more foreign languages.

"They do sound most strange, so very down-to-earth in translation, don't they?" remarked Jessie. "Though I'm sure they themselves never worried about what their names sounded like or meant in other languages." She paused. "What's in a name anyway?" she concluded.

Pickle put down his coffee-cup and said, "Ah! Some people worry terribly about their names. I know one case of a girl who hated her surname, and if she had not with time cured herself of that particular obsession, she could have ended up being – well, quite miserable, I suppose. Unnecessarily so," he added.

"Unless I'm much mistaken, this is an introduction to a story," said Jessie.

"Well... I suppose... Yes," admitted Pickle.

"Does it have a happy ending?" Jessie wanted to know.

"Oh yes. Definitely a happy ending."

"Then go ahead," Jessie decreed. "We're listening."

Andrea flung down her schoolbag, in the manner of a provoked medieval knight throwing down a particularly aggrieved gauntlet, and flopped onto the settee. She was barely able to keep back the tears.

"Whatever's the matter, dear?" asked her mother, anxiously.

"School was horrid today."

"Oh? Why?"

"They've been teasing me again. They always do. They keep on. Every day. I hate it! And I hate them!" She finally burst into tears of helpless rage.

Her mother came and sat down beside her, putting a comforting arm round her twelve –year old daughter's shoulders.

"What did they tease you about, sweetheart? Who was teasing you?"

"Everybody. All the time. Even my friends. Even Jilly. Huh! They call themselves my friends, but they join in. They always make fun of my name. Why do we have to have such a stupid surname? Why? I hate it!"

Mrs Tilterkettle sighed. This had been the one and only thing that had caused her to hesitate – and that only slightly, just as Caesar must have hesitated before venturing to dip his toes into the Rubicon – before agreeing to marry the man who had proposed to her, the man with whom she was so deeply in love, who was such fun to be with. Somehow, he had always managed to make light of what might have made lesser mortals miserable, this strange surname. It was David Tilterkettle's unruffled, good-humoured and eminently practical attitude that had enabled his wife to face life with what she could so easily have regarded as a burden and a handicap, socially at least. But it hadn't mattered at all in the end. Everyone accepted her for what she was, and she had never been conscious of anyone making fun of her name. On that score she need never have worried at all. Of course, it was easier for a grown up than for a schoolgirl, she realised, and now their second daughter was evidently experiencing the problem. It had to be faced.

"Listen, darling," she said calmly. "Daddy and I don't let it worry us, do we? After all, it isn't something to be ashamed of. We even think of it as making us all, in a way, a bit... well, different. And special. In any case, it's not going to be your name forever. One day," and she paused to smile encouragingly at Andrea, "You'll meet a handsome young man, you'll fall in love and get married, and then you won't be a Tilterkettle any more. You'll be Mrs Smith, or Mrs Brown, or Mrs Jones, or something else very ordinary. Now, how about that?"

"It'll be a lot better than being a Tilterkettle! At least, nobody will make fun of me any more. I'll marry anyone, anyone at all who has a proper surname, and I'll never, never" – she almost screamed the word – "marry any man with a silly name. Never! Never! I really mean it! Never!"

Andrea having thus established unequivocally that her position on this issue was not open to negotiation, Mrs Tilterkettle wisely decided to pursue a different tack in her efforts to cheer her daughter.

"You worry too much about it, dear," she replied calmly. "What does a name matter anyway? It's the person that's important, not what he or she is called."

"Why don't my so-called friends know that?" retorted Andrea petulantly.

"They will make less of it if you do," counselled her mother. "Just don't let it get to you. Try laughing with them and they'll laugh with you, not at you. They'll grow up and so will you, and you'll see what a very small thing a name is."

Andrea was however only partially comforted, and when her elder sister Clare came home from work, Andrea made a point of airing her grievances to her, in search of sympathy and reassurance. Clare, being a few years older and being made of sterner stuff than her young sister, virtually repeated the advice that their mother had given. Andrea was convinced that nobody understood her or appreciated the difficulties under which she lived out her young life, and she went to bed that night in a miserable state, grumbling about the unfairness of life in general for a twelve –year old girl, and in particular the seemingly arbitrary way in which silly surnames were handed out, as though they were free samples of some new washing powder.

She was still harbouring this unfortunately exaggerated grievance when, a year or so later, Clare announced her engagement to her boyfriend of long standing. His name was John Smith. They were married in due course, and Andrea was Clare's bridesmaid. All through the wedding and subsequent festivities Andrea's main emotion was envy; this was centred entirely on her sister who was acquiring a 'sensible' surname – a Tilterkettle no more. She was now Mrs John Smith. Her husband was, in fact, a very ordinary sort of chap. He had a steady respectable job in a bank, was clean-shaven, rarely laughed, always had his hair neatly combed, never spoke out of turn or wore scruffy clothes, and never exceeded the speed limit when driving his car. He never, in short, did anything to offend anyone.

Still nursing the large and greasy chip that had found its niche in life on her shoulder, Andrea in time left school and went off to college. There were social events to be anticipated, and Mr and Mrs Tilterkettle told themselves that as their younger daughter grew up, saw more of the world and met more people, she would be able to put the whole question of her pet phobia into perspective. They were accordingly delighted when Andrea, in one of her weekly letters home, reported on the wonderful time she'd had at the Saturday night dance at the college. She had met a charming young man whom, she told them, she would be very pleased to meet again, should fate ever cause their paths to cross again at some point.

Andrea's next letter brought the news that the young man had indeed duly arranged for fate to cause their paths to cross again, and that he had taken her out. Andrea was both flattered and pleased by the attention he showed toward her. Furthermore his name, she informed her parents, was Stewart Duncan.

"Aha!" exclaimed her father, with a hearty laugh. "You see? Stewart Duncan! That should please our little girl, eh? There's nothing wrong with a good old-fashioned Scottish name like that, is there?"

And off he went to work, chortling away to himself, and repeating the name Stewart Duncan. He was, of course, very fond of his daughter and wanted her to be happy.

This happiness alas was doomed, as surely as that of the Trojans when they dragged the wooden horse inside their city's walls, not to last. It turned out, as Andrea pointed out in her next letter, that there was more to her beau's name than she had been led to believe: true, he was Stewart Duncan, but these were only two of his Christian names. His full name was Stewart Duncan Rudgwick Tweddlethirk, which as Andrea wrote, "is, however you say it, almost as bad as Tilterkettle. So I'm not seeing him again. I wonder what his school friends used to make of him!"

"Oh dear. Out of the frying-pan, etc., by the sound of it," commented her father. "Ah well, let's hope she'll have better luck next time."

"There will be another time, I hope?" his wife asked, with just a touch of anxiety.

"Of course there will! She's only young. Now don't you start worrying."

It was shortly after this that, out of the blue, Andrea received a letter from Jilly, her old school friend. Jilly had been the extrovert of the class, a bubbly, gossipy girl who wore, as the saying goes, her heart on her sleeve. She was the sort of girl who is always ready to try anything and not be afraid of making a fool of herself. Jilly had often said after she became seriously aware of the opposite sex that she would marry any man she fancied, regardless of what his name was. She had made this comment to Andrea on frequent occasions, in an attempt perhaps to persuade her that names don't really matter. Since they had gone their separate ways after leaving school, Andrea had sometimes wondered whether Jilly had found the soulmate she was so eager to meet, and if so whether she was now saddled with the sort of surname from which she, Andrea, would run a mile. Now she knew – the purpose of Jilly's letter was not only to renew an old interrupted friendship but also to tell Andrea the happy news that she had just become engaged to the most marvellous man in the whole world. His name was Michael Jones.

"You must, absolutely must," wrote Jilly, "come to our wedding. We don't yet know when it will be, but you will promise to be there, won't you?"

With a sigh, Andrea finished reading the letter and put it down on the table. Some people had all the luck. And others had none at all. Why, she wondered, couldn't she meet some wonderful man with a sensible name?

Ah well.

Four years had passed, and Andrea was now working in the local office of a large company. She was happy enough in her work without exactly relishing it, was an aunt twice over to her sister's children, and godmother to Jilly's second child.

One day, as she was secretly brooding over her maiden state, a handsome young sales rep walked into the office. He apologised profusely for disturbing her, having clearly walked in through the wrong door, but the outcome of their brief encounter was that he came back the following week, having made a point this time of deliberately coming in at the wrong door. This second visit was less quickly over; he stayed to chat for a while with Andrea, and before he left he had invited her out for a meal, followed by an evening out at the theatre. He introduced himself without ceremony or fuss.

"Call me Maff," he said as he departed, giving her a flirtatious wink.

Funny name, thought Andrea – though who am I to talk? Maybe it's short for Matthew if he lisps, or perhaps he can't pronounce 'th' properly. Can't be that though, because he said 'theatre' clearly enough. Odd. But never mind. In any case I'll call him Maff, if that's what he wants.

Maff, poor fellow, was destined not to survive their first and only date. When Andrea learned not only that Maff was short for Mafeking – and that's bad enough on its own, she thought – but also that his surname was Ditherstrottle, it was more than her pride would allow her to take. Mafeking Ditherstrottle! When she said it to herself the poor girl blenched. Seeing her unpromising reaction to his confession, he tried to make light of his misfortune by joking about it.

"I can only assume," he reasoned, "that my parents, having inflicted a daft surname on me, thought that they owed it to me to give men a daft Christian name as well."

He laughed a hollow laugh, while Andrea smiled weakly. His effort at wit was all in vain, and the poor chap was consigned mercilessly to the waste-bin of Andrea's boyfriends of short standing.

"I see our new neighbours have moved in at last," announced Mrs Tilterkettle one evening. "The van was there this morning, and it was gone by mid-afternoon."

"What are they like, the new neighbours?" asked her husband.

"Well, I haven't actually seen anyone – apart from the removal men, that is. I'm glad the bungalow's been taken, after all this time."

The bungalow next door to the Tilterkettles' house had in fact been standing empty for the last three months, since the previous occupants, a retired couple, had moved out to go and live with their daughter in a neighbouring town.

"I hope we shall get on with them as well as we did with the Renshaws," said Mr Tilterkettle. "They were a lovely couple, and we do miss them, don't we? Still, I expect you'll be seeing something of the new folks soon enough, my dear."

"I'll keep my eyes open, and see if they need any help," replied Mrs Tilterkettle. "I could invite them in for a cup of coffee if I see them tomorrow."

"I suppose…" mused Andrea, half to herself, "that it's too much to hope that there's a decent young man, who's good-looking, intelligent, interesting, and who has a sense of humour. And," she added firmly, "who has a sensible surname."

"We'll see, my dear, in time," replied Mr Tilterkettle, reflecting that it would be ironical if Andrea, having failed to meet a 'suitable' young man during her years away at college, were to find a soulmate on, so to speak, her own doorstep.

The next day, when her husband and her daughter came home from work, Mrs Tilterkettle was able to inform them that there was only one new neighbour, and she had been chatting to him over a cup of coffee. He was, she told them, a most likeable, friendly young man, very good-looking, about the same age as Andrea, with an interesting job that involved him in quite a lot of travel to exciting places.

"What's his name?" asked Andrea, with an eagerness that was not lost on her parents.

"Peter Brown," replied Mrs Tilterkettle. "Andrea dear, as it's Saturday tomorrow, why don't you pop round in the morning to say hello to him, and to introduce yourself? He'll probably be very pleased to meet somebody else of his own age."

"I shall do just that," smiled Andrea.

She was as good as her word. Having brushed her hair carefully and applied her make-up with particular attention, she presented herself at Peter Brown's front door. However, her parents were surprised and disappointed to see her return, after a half an hour or so, with a very long face.

"Well?" asked her mother. "Did you like him?"

"He's not on his own," replied Andrea, ignoring the question. "His partner is moving in with him in a fortnight."

"Oh. So he has a steady girlfriend?"

"No, mum. His partner is called Winston. He has a steady boyfriend."

Time went on, and Andrea was now in her late twenties. Time, she thought, to take stock of her situation. She had begun to reflect, with a fair measure of regret, how much she liked or might have grown to like on further acquaintance the men she had rejected purely on account of their surnames. It had become, she found herself admitting, a foolish obsession with her, a bad habit, a prejudice that was now deep-seated and would not just go away unless she forced it to do so. Did a name really matter as she had always maintained? Perhaps her mother had been right when all those years ago, she had said that an unusual surname was not something to be ashamed of. Maybe it really did, or should, make you feel special? Maybe it was true that people didn't even notice? But then, her mother had said that Andrea would not remain a Tilterkettle forever; that she would meet and fall in love with a handsome young man whom she'd marry, and so put her stupid name behind her. After all, her sister had done precisely that. Yes, but her name was now Smith, and what if all the handsome young men whom Andrea herself might meet had names that were as silly as Tilterkettle? That certainly seemed to be the way of things so far. But then again, if she kept on turning down good men because of her attitude to their names, she would have only herself to blame if she ended up 'on the shelf', and she didn't want that. She was made more acutely aware of such a possibility when her young colleague Sharon announced to the office in general that her boyfriend had popped the question and that she had accepted. They all rushed to congratulate Sharon on her engagement. The couple were to be married in the summer, and Sharon would become Mrs Geoffrey Williams. Andrea felt mortified. Why, she asked herself yet again, did other girls have all the luck?

But was it really just a question of luck? Andrea had at last to admit that the name was not important. What was it that Shakespeare once said? Something about a rose smelling just as sweet, whatever you called it.

Anyway, shortly after her twenty eighth birthday, Tony came into her life. They were instantly drawn to each other. They enjoyed each other's company without reserve or shyness. They shared common interests. In short, they were made for each other.

They had been courting for about six months when Andrea made a resolution. By this time she was so sure of their love for each other that she decided to say yes as soon as Tony proposed, as she was certain he would. This was, in fact, a very wise decision on her part. Tony however had a streak of caution in his make-up; not that he was timid or unadventurous, or any sort of stick-in-the-mud. But he did want to be sure. So he kept Andrea waiting for a few months before he finally asked her to marry him. She had no hesitation in accepting and, to the delight of everyone concerned, especially her parents, they were married the following spring.

They're blissfully happy; neither has ever for a moment entertained the slightest bit of regret about their being man and wife.

But I cannot help smiling to myself, as I wonder what thoughts go through Andrea's mind each time she looks at her two daughters and reflects on how fortunate she is to be Mrs Anthony Hannibal Trigthorpe Tilterpott.

"So there you are, Jessie," Pickle concluded. "You asked earlier what's in a name. Does that little tale help you to answer the question?"

The happy ending that Pickle had managed to engineer for his story had brought smiles to the faces of the entire company, and even a short round of spontaneous applause.

"On the evidence of what we've just heard," Jessie answered, "I'd say the answer is that a name means absolutely nothing. Mind you, Andrea did her best to make herself miserable over it, didn't she?"

"It's another aspect of what old Horace, the Roman poet, used to crack on about," said Velly, adding a serious intellectual note to the proceedings. "You know, the idea of the 'aurea mediocritas', the golden mean, the avoidance of extremes. Because young Andrea's attitude was an extreme one, wasn't it?"

"Well," put in Traffy. "She was only young when she first started hating her name, so it became a habit that grew with her. She was just unfortunate in that she was teased when she was, and that she reacted in the wrong way, so that her attitude became an ingrained habit."

"Hurrah for Hannibal, anyway," said Pickle.

"What are you lads going to play now?" asked Jessie. "While I'm washing up these cups and plates."

"Well now, let's see what we've got," replied Velly. He rummaged through a pile of music, but paused suddenly.

"I think," he said, "that my favourite horrible translation of a name must be either 'Roger Lionhorse' or 'Marius Newcastle-German'. Both Italian, of course. But as far as piano trios are concerned I think we need to look elsewhere."

Traffy, grappling quietly with the problem of converting into Italian the two names that Velly had mentioned, soon came up with Ruggiero Leoncavallo and Mario Castelnuovo-Tedesco.

"Bravo!" cried Velly.

"Too clever by half," grunted Pickle. "Let's play something. By which I mean music, not childish linguistic games. Or silly names."

"How about Schubert's Bflat trio?" enquired Velly, who had just unearthed it and was waving it aloft. "Now that's not got a silly name, has it?"

"I'll settle for that," agreed Pickle.

"An excellent choice," said Traffy.

"Leave the door open so that I can listen," ordered Jessie, as she went out, carrying the tray.

Isaac of Musten Parva

"Were you ever an autograph hunter in your misspent youth?" Jessie asked Velly.

"Well, I did once –" he broke off as the doorbell rang.

Traffy and Pickle had arrived for an afternoon of music-making.

"Jessie was just asking," Velly explained to his friends, "if I had ever been an autograph hunter."

"Well, were you?" Jessie insisted.

"Only in a perfunctory sort of way," Velly replied. "I have never gone out of my way to get the signature of some famous person, but if I happened to meet one and happened to have a pen and paper on me, I –"

"So we are to assume that you never collected any autographs," concluded Traffy with a laugh.

"Just so. Actually, I was more keen on cigarette cards or Dinky toys."

"I was a great one for marbles," put in Pickle. "In fact, I had quite a big collection. All colours, all sizes."

Jessie informed the menfolk that she had once amassed a sizeable collection of postcards, but that they'd all disappeared, over the years. Then she asked Traffy what his particular weakness had been.

"Oh, nothing so ordinary as cigarette cards, or marbles or toy motorcars," he answered. "What really interested me from my teenage years onwards was collecting pub names."

"You mean," chortled Pickle, "like 'Red Lion', or 'King's Head', 'The Traveller's Rest', and so on?"

"Well, yes. But I preferred the more exotic ones. Wherever I travelled when I was younger, I used to look out for unusual names. If there was a story behind the name, and there was, surprisingly often, then so much the better."

"For example?"

"Let me think, now. Ah, yes. How about 'The Cap and Candles'?"

"Most unusual," agreed Jessie. "And are you telling us that there's a story behind that name?"

"Definitely," replied Traffy.

"Right," said Jessie, decisively. "You three chaps do a bit of music-making now, and I'll come back later with some afternoon tea and biscuits, and it'll be storytime."

Nobody chose to argue with that.

"You know," Traffy began, "how rural communities have at times tended to be a bit narrow-minded in their outlook, and resistant to change in a way that city folks would not be. Stubbornly intolerant of outsiders coming in, too?" Well, some eight hundred years ago, the hamlet of Musten Parva was just such a community. It was not a place where anyone might imagine he could just move into from outside and settle in amicably with the people who already lived there. A man called Isaac once brought his family to Musten Parva, and they very soon found there was no welcome for outsiders such as themselves. It was in the first place their unwitting misfortune that they happened to take up residence in the cottage by the riverside that had become vacant following the death of its owner, the widow Nettlecorn. Mistress Nettlecorn had been one of the best-loved people in the parish, a cheerful old body who lived alone and independent, was unfailingly eager to help others, always ready with a smile and a friendly word, ever busy and still active as a midwife until the day she died. Her passing was sincerely lamented by all. Her few possessions, since she remained poor, were soon disposed of and her cottage stood empty and almost revered as a shrine. That was until Isaac arrived. He came ahead of his wife and their little daughter in search of work. Nobody knew why had he come there; it was rumoured that he was running away from somebody or something, yet it was soon noticed that he shunned the church, the obvious refuge of one seeking sanctuary – at least in the first instance. He chief concern had been to find work, of any kind, and this he soon found in the fields and on the farms, since it was late summer and the harvest was due. He kept himself to himself and disappeared each evening on his own, as if fleeing from contact with a hostile society. No one knew where he slept at night, but he was an assiduous and punctual worker.

The feeling of resentment against the three strange outsiders, who had dared to come and make their home in the very cottage where Widow Nettlecorn had lived and held sway, was almost tangible – and a bad omen. Isaac was soon being talked about as a man of mystery. There was something different about him – not physically, since he was much the same as other men in his looks. But he never mixed, never took part in any activity with the other men, but just got on quietly with his work.

It was Goody Clifford who, returning home one Friday evening from a visit to her sister in a neighbouring hamlet, brought some disquieting news to her husband. In passing in front of Widow Nettlecorn's, as it was still called, she had yielded to curiosity and peeped inside.

"There were candles burning, Sturdy," she told her man. "Only, they was all in a row, on a sort of rack thing. The man had a strange little hat on, and he were mumblin' strange words... As if they was prayin'... As if, like, in church."

"But 'tis Friday, woman. Who prays on a Friday night?"

"And he had, like, a sort of shawl on. And then the candles..."

"A shawl, you say? Well, maybes he were cold. 'Tis November just now. That'll be why they had candles lit, for sure. 'Twas dark, after all."

"But who can afford candles? We have to make manage with rush tapers, if we're lucky. But these weren't candles meant to light a room. There was a strange sort of..." She groped for the word 'atmosphere'. "I tell you, I don't like it."

"You've too much imagination, woman. Leave a body alone. He's not harmin' anyone. Let him be."

Unfortunately, Sturdy Clifford's words had exactly the opposite effect to the one desired. Sturdy himself was not a man given to meddling in matters outside his own immediate concern; nor was he disposed to see harm where there most likely was none, unless or until it should actually touch him. Of all the parishioners, he was the one most inclined to live and let live – an attitude that Goody at times felt bordered on indolence. Now, she had more imagination – too much, if her husband was to be believed – and having been disturbed in her mind by her brief encounter with the doings of Isaac and his family, she was not prepared to let the matter rest. Accordingly, she wasted no time the next morning in seeking out her neighbour Meg Trattles, and recounting to her all that she had witnessed in the cottage by the river. Needless to say, she embroidered a few details and produced a dramatic narrative. For her efforts, she was rewarded by the interest shown by Meg, and by the suitably incredulous expression on her face as the tale was unfolded.

"We must tell the priest," the good lady declared firmly, in reverential tones. "For he has learnin', and he knows many things that the likes of us cannot fathom. Besides," – and she lowered her voice to a conspiratorial whisper – "if there should be witchcraft, or dealings with the devil or the like in our village, 'tis only the priest can help us. The Lord have mercy on us."

Thus was Isaac condemned on two counts: firstly, the connection was soon established between the mysterious newcomer and Satan. Secondly, the priest was able to tell them that Isaac was a Jew.

Within a very short space of time all the women of the hamlet knew why Isaac did not go to church like all good Christian folk, and the men, upon their return from their work, were immediately informed.

First reactions carried; among both male and female sections of the community there were those who expressed frank outrage that such a person should dare to presume to live among them. Others such as Sturdy Clifford were less excited, and were prepared to give the man a chance and judge him by his deeds rather than on mere prejudice. This latter group formed a quiet, tolerant minority. Had the parish as a whole followed their example, Isaac and his family might have lived in peace in the community indefinitely.

"I don't like having Jews for neighbours," muttered Meg as she and Goody bent over their washing. "We all know 'twas the Jews as killed Jesus. They're heathens, and a body can't trust heathens."

"'Tis said they have money," Goody replied, scrubbing at her linen, "and when folks have money..."

In truth, Isaac was not a wealthy man – the very reverse. Although many others of his religion in the towns and cities of England were rich enough to be important lenders of money to the king and his barons, and to his warlords assembling armies for the crusades, Isaac himself was a refugee from the persecution suffered by many Jews. In theory, the king was giving a measure of protection to the Jews in return for the loan of their money; in practice, his officials, and even the church itself, found it more convenient to look the other way when a Jew was robbed or ill treated. It was indeed true that Jews had money, money that they put to usury; it was equally true that there were many men of power and influence who, though they were eager enough to borrow Jewish money on a grand scale, were much less eager to pay back what they owed when their debts were called in. Consequently, a good deal of ill treatment was meted out to the Jews by creditors who, sacrificing an inconvenient conscience to their resentment at being beholden to the despised usurers, chose to settle their debts by inflicting exemplary violence on the lenders, while the forces of law and order stood by and allowed this summary justice to take its course. Many a Jew found it wiser to write off even substantial debts than to attempt to pursue his claims, knowing that whatever might be the letter of the law, its spirit was decidedly hostile to him. Isaac, like so many of his kind, had been so relentlessly pursued and harassed by powerful debtors determined not to pay back what they owed him, that he had finally fled the city in fear of his life and had come to seek refuge, virtually penniless, in the isolation of Musten Parva.

At first then, an uneasy truce reigned in the tiny village. There were no complaints concerning Isaac's work, and it was as if the villagers were biding their time, waiting to see what sort of person their new neighbour might turn out to be, or perhaps waiting for a suitable moment to turn on him. The spread of the news that he was a Jew proved to be a turning point in the way he was treated. Throughout the months of their first winter in Musten Parva, Isaac and his family were made to feel outcasts, and this was done in various unpleasant ways. Clods of earth, hardened by the frost, were thrown at them. They were jeered at. Even, on one occasion, someone threw at Isaac a broken axe-shaft, whose jagged end only just went wide of its unsuspecting target. Nobody came to offer him or his wife and child either food or anything for their material comfort. Indeed they were, on the contrary, subjected to various minor irritations, such as the theft of a pile of firewood that Isaac had gathered against the chill weather. His daughter, each time she showed her face outside the little home, was likely to be subjected to insults and taunts; toys or trinkets were dangled in front of her face to attract her attention and then hastily snatched away as soon as she reacted. The children of the parish became very adept at devising ways of trying to humiliate poor Esther. She quickly learned, however, not to let herself be affected; as Rebecca had pointed out to her, by reacting to the taunts she would merely gratify the mean instincts of her tormentors. She had thus developed the ability to treat her tormentors with the contempt they deserved. Doubtless, the children had their attitude formed for them by the odd comments they heard from time to time from their elders. Beth Simmond, the mother of the dull-witted and loutish Will, and noted gossip, left none of the villagers in any doubt as to how she felt.

"Holy Church says it's not right for good Christian folks to make a living out of the profits of lending money. It's called usury. The good book says 'thou shalt not put thy money to usury'. That's clear enough, it seems to me. Now, the Jews have no respect for the good book or what Holy Church teaches, and 'tis the Jews that practise usury. That means they're heathens, says what you will."

Meg Trattles also had a contribution to make, a contribution that created a big impression among her hearers.

"There'll be witchcraft, aye, and Devil-worship," she informed then. "And 'tis said..." she went on, lowering her voice dramatically. "'Tis said they sacrifice little children."

"Aye, so I've heard tell," echoed another woman, while several others nodded.

Beth went on with her peroration. "We don't want no murderin' heathen here, bringing their ungodly ways, corruptin' and murderin' – aye, murderin' – our little ones. He's wicked, that Jew. Wicked through and through. You mark my words. Him and all his kind."

She looked round to see if anyone wished to contradict her. None did. Despite her reputation for having a ready tongue and for speaking out first and thinking afterwards, all were ready to agree that on this occasion the gossip was in the right. It was no secret that the Jews were moneylenders and that the church frowned on usury as an immoral practice. One or two souls like Sturdy Clifford shook their heads, but said and did nothing in defence of Isaac. As the days and weeks went by, the attitude of the villagers hardened inexorably against the innocent refugees who sheltered in their midst. If any knew, none saw fit to tell Beth Simmonds or those who heeded her that it was very often Jewish money that financed the building of the great churches and monastic buildings of the land.

One evening, on his way home from the strip where he had laboured all day, Isaac was met by Will Simmonds, who planted himself firmly in front of the Jew and barred his way.

"Why do you stay here, Jew? You're not wanted – you or any of your kind," growled Will.

Isaac smiled faintly, a patient, long-suffering smile.

"But, my friend, I do no harm to anyone. All I ask is –"

Will cut him short with a vicious blow across the mouth.

"Be on your way, moneybags!" he snarled. "Son of Satan! Christ killer!"

Then he spat in Isaac's face, turned on his heel, and left him, with a mocking laugh.

For a moment the Jew stood rooted to the spot, pondering the tragic irony of Will's words. Money? He had little enough of that. Christ killer? How could such a carelessly flung insult be relevant to him? Why was religion allowed to poison human relations in this way? Isaac had no answers to these and other questions that had always plagued his people, and had now come to torment him. Sadly, he wiped his face and continued on his way.

Not long after that incident, early in spring, little Esther was set upon by Will Simmonds and came home tearful, bruised and bleeding.

"He said it was just a warning," she sobbed, "and that he'd do worse if he had to."

For Rebecca and Isaac, this was a new and disturbing development. The taunts, the insults, the indignities and humiliation, although they had caused the family much mental distress, had been bearable because they had had to be. But now physical violence had brought a new dimension to their suffering. With sinking hearts, Isaac and Rebecca began to dread what might happen next. Both realised the futility of any appeal to the official representatives of justice. Secretly, Isaac, normally the most patient and gentle of men, swore that he himself would exact his own revenge in his own way when a suitable occasion might present itself, or be engineered. Yet, as he daily pondered in vain how, alone with his Rebecca and with the world against him, he might find redress, or at least a sympathetic ear, a more horrifying tragedy was inflicted on them. Little Esther could not be found. Rebecca, seeing that the afternoon light was fading, and since Esther did not respond to her call, had become anxious for the little girl's safety. She was still missing when Isaac came home at the end of his day's work, even though Rebecca had been out to look for her. Sick with a dreadful foreboding, Isaac went out immediately in search of his daughter. He returned after darkness had fallen, bearing the lifeless body of the little girl in his arms. In a broken voice he told Rebecca how he had found the pathetic little corpse down by the river after seeing shreds of her clothing clinging to some bushes.

"She was just... lying there... So innocent... Our little Esther," he stammered. "So sweet... So... holy." The word choked him. "How can people be so cruel, so... wicked, so... evil?"

Rebecca stared at the horrific injuries inflicted on her daughter and fainted.

As a further insult to add to their grief, they were obliged to bury the child themselves, secretly and after dark, behind the cottage: the land was not even theirs to use as they wished, and so the discovery that they had used it for a private burial would have had them evicted immediately. The spot of earth where their precious only child lay would be forever a reminder to them of how their Christian neighbours had treated them. Isaac and Rebecca never did find out that Esther had been dragged away by Will Simmonds who, lacking the intelligence to question his mother's vicious and ill-considered remarks, was single-handedly pursuing his own private campaign of hatred and violence against the Jewish family. He had tormented and humiliated Esther before beating her to death.

This tragedy broke Isaac's spirit; he no longer had the stomach to stand against the treatment meted out to his family. Rebecca, for her part, went about with eyes permanently red through weeping tears of unutterable distress. Each tried for little Esther's sake to comfort the other, but neither was able at such a time to find an answer to the un-asked question – what was the point of carrying on living?

Then malicious gossip of a horrifying and sinister kind began to spread within a few days of Esther's murder. The child's absence was noticed, and good matter for gossip was made of it.

"Disappeared, she has. Vanished. And we may wonder where she's disappeared to, I daresay," said Meg to the huddle of wives gathered round her. "Well now, you remember how

Beth said that the Jews sacrificed little children for their devil worship –"

"Doubtless they've sacrificed their own child!" Beth almost screamed, butting in. A cackle of vicious laughter went round the group.

"Ay, you did say so, Beth."

"'Tis surely so."

"Their own child. Their very own flesh and blood."

"We must watch our own little ones closely, or else they'll suffer the same fate."

Thus infanticide, and that of his own daughter, was added to the list of crimes of which Isaac was judged guilty.

Gradually however, the sorrow, the misery, the distress that the bereaved parents constantly felt began in Isaac's heart to harden. A strong surge of indignation rose within this mild and sensitive man, and an urge for revenge became his consuming passion. It would be revenge against these smug, self-righteous Christian people who despised him and his kind because of some unreasoning and disproportionate prejudice. The form that his revenge would take must strike a blow at the Christian faith, must insult it, must arouse in the parishioners the same indignation that Isaac himself had come to feel. He vowed that he would achieve this, even if he had to lose his life in so doing.

It was Easter Day. Dawn had barely begun to cast its first faint glow across the sky, but Will Simmonds was up and about. Under cover of the dark he had set his traps the previous evening, and he was now off on a secret and dangerous mission to see if he had caught anything for the stockpot. As he crept warily along, he became aware that another person was also abroad. This other figure was making its way furtively through the village, and was evidently as keen as Will himself not to be observed. Intrigued, Will began to follow, taking great care to make no sound. As the mysterious figure neared the church, it turned round as if to check that nobody was following. To his astonishment, Will saw that the man he was shadowing was Isaac, and that Isaac was actually going into the church. His curiosity now fully aroused, Will closed stealthily on the man, and from the open doorway silently watched Isaac's every movement. The Jew looked quickly round the church in the gathering light. Reassured by the total silence, he walked up to where the Bible lay, picked it up, then gently replaced it. He did the same think with the chalice on the side-table by the altar. He went up to a stone crucifix, stared at it for a moment then, watched all the time by Will, he hurried through a small door and mounted the steps that led up to the bell-tower.

When the priest arrived at the church later on that Easter morning to lead the people in their worship and rejoicing, he found the precious volume of the New Testament a smouldering heap of ashes on the chancel floor.

A stone crucifix had been wrenched off the wall and broken in two.

The holy vessels had been trampled and thrown into the font.

The body of Isaac the Jew was hanging by the neck from a rope attached to a beam in the bell tower. The lifeless eyes gazed balefully down on the desecration that, as the evidence plainly suggested, had been Isaac's last act in this world.

"And that," Traffy concluded, "is the story of Isaac of Musten Parva."

"Powerful stuff," said Velly.

"Mind you," Traffy went on, "it was not Isaac who was responsible for the sacrilege. It just wasn't in his nature. Of course, Will Simmonds never told a soul that it was all his doing. When the villagers saw the damage in the church and the Jew's body hanging there, gazing down on them, they put two and two together –"

"– And made five," put in Pickle.

"Indeed. Then they went off in a body to the cottage and murdered poor Rebecca."

Traffy shook his head, as if despairing of humanity.

"Well," said Jessie, "Isaac did say that he wanted to strike a blow at those smug Christians, and to make them feel as indignant as he felt. I reckon he managed that all right, don't you?"

"Oh yes. But whatever plans he may have had when he went into the church, he clearly could not find it in his heart to be so vindictive."

"Two wrongs don't make a right, eh?"

"Quite. He didn't harm or damage anything in the church. But I think he still got his revenge, even if it did cost him his life."

There was silence for a moment while they all pondered over this tragic tale. Then suddenly, Velly looked up.

"What," he queried, "has this story got to do with that pub name that led up to it, the 'Cap and Candles'?"

"Ah, yes. Well, they were originally Isaac's skull-cap and the menorah, which both somehow found their way into the brewer's family."

"I wonder," mused Pickle, "whether the present landlord knows that."